Karl B. Daniel, *a.k.a. Queen Karlotta*, was born and raised in Olney, Illinois, home of the White Squirrels. It is here that Karl met his Soul brother and comedic comrade, Bradley J. Provines, whom he credits for the completion of this book. Upon graduation from college, armed with only one suitcase and one thousand dollars, Karl dauntlessly took a formidable leap of faith to achieve his dream of living in the one singular sensational city: Manhattan. Karl began to regale his fellow New Yorkers with a variety of zany stories from his childhood. Much to his chagrin, everyone who listened also hysterically laughed, especially when they realized that these 'one of a kind' 'out of this world' tales were tantalizingly true!

Bradley J. Provines, *a.k.a. Princess Provincia*, is also proud to hail from the town famous for White Squirrels. Growing older, some say he is now beginning to resemble the jaunty albino mascot himself in both face and posterior. As a child, Bradley happily escaped into the world of humor brilliantly inspired by entertainment icons known around the globe by one name: Carol, Lucy, Mary, Doris, Barbra, Goldie, Ellen, Johnny, Jane & Bette. Together with his life long friend and partner in comedy, Karl B. Daniel, Bradley views every bizarre experience (and he has attracted a ton of them) as potentially funny material to be joyfully shared like contagious laughter which is unstoppable. That's what this book is all about. Enjoy!

My Brother Married My Sister. Where DO I Sit?

Titillating Tales from White Squirrel Town

by

Karl B. Daniel & Bradley J. Provines

AuthorHouse™
1663 Liberty Drive
Bloomington, IN 47403
www.authorhouse.com
Phone: 1-800-839-8640

First published by AuthorHouse 6/18/2010

ISBN: 978-1-4520-2655-8 (e)
ISBN: 978-1-4520-2653-4 (sc)
ISBN: 978-1-4520-2654-1 (hc)

Library of Congress Control Number: 2010907459

Printed in the United States of America
Bloomington, Indiana

This book is printed on acid-free paper.

For our Mothers'
Mary Jo Provines &
Eleanor Kaye Rice
without whom,
this book would not have
been possible!

We would like
to express our
heartfelt gratitude to
Antonio Fabién León
info@efekto.tv
for his brilliant
cover design!

Our V.I.P. THANK YOUS

Jack & Mary Jo Provines
Percy & Helen Provines
Tony, Melissa & Sophie McDaniel
John Provines & Michelle
Mike & Kristina Provines
Laura & Michael Martin
Michael Provines & Kelly Rubalcaba
Gretchen, Davis Griffin & Aidan Cly
Jane Toennies
Jean Nosbisch
Blake Pyo
Hun-Dong Yu
Jane, Jeff & Tim Bryan
Linette , Kendal & Hannah Thomas
Kay, Ron & Matt Nowak
Gary, Cookie & Shane Amerman
Frank Wagner & Isabella Caputo
Sarah Frahm & Carlos Mora
Ted Ehrhardt & Nina Robinson
Ursula & Chris Caravayo
Kathy Donnelly
Josh (Chiahsi) Yu
Karen Travers
Mechelle Chestnut
Armando Velez
Alethia Johnson
Kim Keller
Bernice Stabile
Jill Merl
Nigel Salmingo
Merton Chinen
Johnson Wang
All my über talented peeps at NYCHHC & the entire CAT Dept: Amy, Barbara, Catherine, Dan, Dana, Einat, Frances, Fred, Jon, Inga, Kristen, Lauren, Marcia, Margaret, Meghan, Monika, Nir, Tomika, Uli & Will.

Kaye Rice
Anita Jones
Charles & Fontella Taylor
Greg & Thomas Rice
Allisa Jones
Bruce Daniel
Mike, Sarah & Silas Daniel
Amanda & Makayla Daniel
Luis Pacheco
A. Maldonado
Stacey Feder & Ricky Seidenberg
Ed Hilla
Ehsan Wahdat
Stephanie Fink & Steve Plakoudas
Sunny Paek
Hank & Kyrene Smulewitz
Erin Augustine
Heather Alexakis
Tim & Patty Wilson
David & Judy Froelke
Paul Berkowitz
Jim Harrigan & Wendi Gibb
Chris Schnaufer
Adeline Tafuri
Anesha Kovalsky
Michael Blakes
Daryl Mattson
Luiz Zorzi
Anthony Connolly
James Bonarrigo
Peter McKeever
Jeannine, Gail & Jay Gustofson
Susan Borwick
Bruce, Irene & Angela Christensen
Antonio Fabien Leon
Eddie Eng
Paula Cohen
Merrie Davis

<u>Message from the Authors:</u>

The authors, Karl B. Daniel & Bradley J. Provines, wish to express their heartfelt gratitude to everyone who helped inspire the creation and completion of this book. While all stories are grounded in real life experience, the names of the characters have been changed for anonymity and comedic effect. We are tremendously thankful for our rich heritage and small town Midwestern values such as integrity, hospitality and loyalty instilled into us by being raised in Olney, Illinois, home of those famously adorable White Squirrels. It is NOT our intention to offend anyone by the content within these pages and we sincerely apologize in advance if anyone's feelings are hurt. It is our united desire to illustrate the undeniably redemptive and healing power of humor. By laughing at our own foibles and humanity, we intend to make you laugh as well. Above all else, please remember this one absolute fact: **<u>IT IS A COMEDY!!</u>** *How you Doin'??*

We're off to see the Squirrels...

Can you imagine a book that begins its fascinating and hysterical journey in a small unassuming Southern Illinois Norman Rockwell picturesque town made Google famous for pink eyed Albino Squirrels and then travels across the country to Manhattan and Hawaii for modern day and just a tad gay, Lucy & Ethel, fall to the floor, laughing 'til you wet your pants adventures? Well kids, here it is! Queen Karlotta & Princess Provincia will not only introduce you to dozens of the wackiest characters ever published but you will also accompany them as they work in Psych. Wards, Nursing Homes, Donut shops and corn fields. (Yes, we said corn!) You will observe them learning how to speak pidgin', parachuting from planes, marching goose step style in a National Band competition, launching professional fireworks from the backyard and even doing a little supernatural ghost whispering, all with unexpected and hilarious results. So come along for the ultimate variety show and comedic ride of your literary life and ask yourself this timely and metaphysically enlightening question: "My brother married my sister. Where DO I sit?"

CONTENTS

"MEET THE CAST OF CHARACTERS"

Empress Adeline
Babette Baboonais
Bobbie Jo Bubbly
Brent Buggerly
Bagunyun Burl
Dundas Calhoun
Kora Carterette
Ethel Clementine
Colleen Cooterpoof
Doris Dawandu
Dolores Dawn Deene
Dr. Doyle Diddler
Doralee Donilly
Melba Drood
Ernie Enyert
Fernie Fennel
Della Faye Frickasee
Forrest Fricker
George Gagoon
Gommorah Gay Goo
Hyacinth Haglet
Jervis Haglet
Harry Hardonya

Helga Horbit
Hazel Horowitz
Erma Junkinette
Sulu Kaaawa
Queen Karlotta
Curt Kukuokopakaulu
Fontella Laduey
Lulaball Limabean
Louise Limpopo
Millie Mennurey
Merl Merkin
Leon Millspow
Mr. Chuckie Moller
Mother-sha-isa-woman
Helena Mowry
Mindy Mae Mullet
Ellen Nellypoot
Norma Nadine Noogan
Verla Pie
Delene Piñata
Peter Poon
Mary Jo Pro-fessional
Princess Provincia

Betsy Ross
Beatrice Sasahuna
Percival Scrotcher
Marbella Burka -Sinduza
Pearl &Sonia Skimmerhorn
Swami Priya Swampwot
Tyrene Trailer
Ursula Underlay
Bernice Wailuku
Wing Dong Wang
Wendy Warthole
Persimmon Yangst

"WHEN *DUNDAS* MET *MINDY*..."

"Welcome to Olney, Illinois: Home of the famous White Squirrels!" This is what the population sign states as you approach my hometown. No, you have not entered the Twilight Zone or some bizarre parallel universe. These righteous rodents truly exist and are Olney's prime tourist attraction. Sure, New York may have its' Statue of Liberty, Broadway and the Empire State Building, but we are abundantly blessed with albino squirrels whose pesky pink eyes pierce right through you. As our revered town mascot, each white squirrel is born with elite status in comparison to the throng of its' darker skinned kin who are cast aside as common vermin. Similar to New York City's Guardian Angels, Olney also has a special swat team task force armed with rifles to patrol and protect the almighty albino. It is indeed a crime punishable by law to shoot, kill or maim one of these cunning Caucasian creatures even during hunting season!

Our family moved to White Squirrel town as I began 8th grade. My mother had recently divorced and was working tirelessly to keep my three brothers and sister fed, dressed and in school. Being a patient, compassionate and generous Soul, our loving matriarch chose to become a licensed foster parent and open her heart and home to a boisterous brood of abused and neglected children of all ages. She also adopted two girls, Mindy Mullet and Tyrene Trailer. At times we had so many children in the household it felt like we were living the story of "The little old woman who lived in a shoe." We weren't exactly "The Brady Bunch" or

"The Partridge Family". Think the ultimate reality series: "Tom and Kaye plus 88!"

Having so many children around certainly kept our lives full of unexpected comedy and drama. One never knew what surprises lurked around the bend, although nothing could prepare us for what would develop years later down the road. My dearly adopted sister, Mindy Mullet, began having romantic feelings for my blood brother, Dundas Calhoun, who in turn had a wild crush on Miss Mindy Mae herself. Love was in the air! They started dating, although no one suspected anything as they were legal siblings. As passions grew and clear heads prevailed, they mutually decided to no longer keep their incestuous relationship secret and soon told the entire family of their desire to be married... *to each other.*

One could imagine our clan's initial reaction to this Earth shattering revelation. Isn't it a nice day for a white squirrel wedding? Would I be asked to sing? Would the family *fork*? As fate would have it, there was one teensy problem. In the eyes of the law, they were legally brother and sister. Though they searched high and low, across the state lines of Illinois, Indiana, Missouri and Ohio, Dundas Calhoun and his pending perky bride, the mesmerizing Mindy Mullet, could not procure the legitimate matrimonial services of a preacher, priest, bishop, rabbi, judge or Imam to perform the ceremony. Even Elvis would not leave the building to touch this one.

Alas, have no fear, Kentucky is here! Good old Paducah comes through in a pinch for sibling nuptials! The wedding was on. Hallelujah! One trivial point of marital etiquette concerned me. Having been a guest at many prior weddings, I was now a tad confused. On which side of the church would I be placed? Let's see. Friends and family of the groom go here, the bride's peeps go there. Hmmm. I exclaimed aloud, "My brother married my sister! Where do I sit?" Doesn't life offer us the most sublimely ridiculous riddles to solve? Save me the aisle seat, please!

"And Then a *SHE-RO* Comes Along!"

I was born in Clay City, Hellinoise (pop. 962). At age 13, we moved to the neighboring metropolis of Olney, a town whose singular claim to record holding fame was the fact that hundreds of ALBINO squirrels chose to make "ALL-KNEE" exclusively their abode. Could it be that my new hometown was so racist that even the rodents were white?

I began 8th grade with everything in the world going for me. I only had two looming concerns. I was flamboyant and I was fat! Flamboyant as in Boy George stranded in Green Acres. Fat as in the only rolls I could do without effort in P.E. class were Hostess and Little Debbie.

My favorite outfit was a pair of electric orange polyester pants topped with a loud zipped down shirt with gigantic printed windmills. I resembled a 300 lb. Dutch boy on mescaline. Imagine my popularity that first day of Junior High. Let us remember 4 key ingredients that composed my first impression: Fat, flamboyant, orange and windmills.

To this day, I have a photograph of myself in this retro ensemble along with my 3 brothers, Bruce, Mike and 9 month old Greg. When I show people this picture and ask them to find me in the shot, it becomes an insurmountable challenge as they inevitably point to each of my 3 brothers in succession. I respond, "No, no, and no!" Then I am always asked, "Well, where the heck are you and who is the humongous heifer woman in hideous tangerine holding the adorable baby?"

"That," I answer, "is me! Thanks!"

On the disaster spectrum, my 1st day of 8th grade ranks somewhere between the elections of George W. Bush and Hurricane Katrina. I was shoved into lockers and swirled into skanky gym toilets. I was called every name but my own. The kids would torment me saying, "Look, everyone, here comes fat fairy faggot fruit freak!" Say that 5 times fast. "Fat fairy faggot fruit freak!" My classroom seat would be secretly adorned with chalk dust, a lively assortment of thumb tacks and gobs of saliva soaked chicle.

I was in Jr. High hell and desperately needed to find a way out! I survived by escaping into the world of television fantasy series starring super heroines. I became obsessed with Wonder Woman, Shazam, Mother Nature and Isis. I meticulously memorized the dialogue. "Elders steed, strong and wise, appear before my seeking eyes. SHAZAM! Zephyr winds which blow on high, lift me now so I might fly, Almighty ISIS!"

Like a volt of electricity, the solution to all my problems struck me! I would morph Shazam, Wonder Woman, Mother Nature and Isis into one super heroine. I would inherit all of their powers and be able to ward off my tormentors who teased and taunted me. My mind leapt into warp speed. It was time to create my own costume combining all 4 dynamic divas into one, my own SHE-RO!

First came Shazam, with revealing cherry red tights and matching cape attached to my magical golden rope. I super glued a yellow lightning bolt onto the back of the cape. Who needs Harry Potter? Over my Shazam tights, I wore my Wonder Woman red, white and blue skirt. Patriotic to the core, kids. Wrists and upper arms were accessorized with Isis bracelets. My forehead pendant was striking emerald green. Mother Nature completed the outfit with her beautiful leaves carefully collected from our yard and strategically sewn onto my costume.

Ta-da! It was finished. I put it on and looked myself up and down in my mother's full length mirror. I couldn't believe my eyes: A 300 lb. super heroine, Mother-Sha-Isa-Woman was born! And then, in the midst of White Squirrel chaos, with perfect timing, a *SHE-RO* came along!

"*B.* on the Ball!"

"Please help me! I don't know what to do.", I muttered to my thirteen year old self. My stepfather walked into my room and said gleefully, "B., I enrolled you for 8th grade football. You start next week. Isn't that exciting?"

"B.", you see, was my nickname ascribed to me as a toddler, taken from my middle name, Burton. The general topic of sports was not exactly my forte. There were just too many balls involved. I couldn't recall if a football was the round bouncy one or the oblong shaped leather object adorned with fancy stitching. I did know that one was played inside a gymnasium and the other in a field of dirt. Stepfather clarified that I would indeed be outside, running about and thrashing into other people who were attempting to score. The only parts of the Super Bowl I enjoyed were the commercials and nachos supreme.

My football debut was only a couple days away and I was petrified. I weighed the same as the goal post and had the dexterity of a sloth receiving S.S.I. The last time I bent over to touch my toes, six school children went missing. In order to calm my nerves, I vividly imagined I would actually be performing in an elegant Broadway musical instead of going to a boring, smelly ball practice. My stepfather drove me to what I would forever christen as "rehearsal".

I was stunned to witness the strength, fitness and flexibility of my fellow cast members. The director approached and said it was time for our daily warm up drills and calisthenics. Was this method acting, Southern Illinois style? The mere thought of exercise made my insides queasy. Did anyone have a case of Oreos I could borrow? He blew his shiny stainless steel whistle and motioned for us to sprint around and around. I was not accustomed to being a ride at Disney. I literally thought I was going to hurl. Considering the fact that my tender thighs were the size of Mt. Kilimanjaro, the act of walking would prompt a rosy rash to form on my inner sanctum.

I put one thunderous foot forward and started to run. Every actor whirled past me at least five times. As I felt planet Earth rumble on each of my steps, I suddenly realized I was the only person still galloping like an old nelly equestrian. The rest of the cast was joyously scrimmaging in the theatre. Huffing and puffing, my horrific dash finally ended. Glancing at my prized "Sleeping Beauty" watch, the time was now ten p.m. The director yelled, "Great first day. Hit the showers." The only thing I wanted to hit was the golden arches and a well deserved happy meal or three.

The following evening it was time to begin rehearsing our 'take downs', whatever they were. We divided into two groups on opposite sides of the stage.

We formed a line and were told to run and tackle the opposing actor. A classic tune from "South Pacific" popped into my head. I sang, "I'm gonna wash that man right out of my hair and send him on his way!" This song filled me with strength I never knew I possessed. I darted immediately towards the beefiest boy in the play. Although he resembled a lumbering giant, I fearlessly wrapped my arms under his huge heifer sized hamstrings, simultaneously pulling, pushing and prancing until this 'beauty' was able to take down that massive mess of a 'beast'. The cast chanted my name. The stage manager remarked my tour de force performance was worthy of a Tony nomination. I was on cloud nine, knowing I had stopped the show cold!

Opening night had arrived and our director was casting the leads. Unfortunately, my name was not chosen but I was anxiously waiting in the wings as the understudy. Watching the same scenes became quite tedious. Quickly, I was summoned to perform as the star was injured and they needed me to substitute for the acclaimed wide receiver. Well, girl, I was certainly wide but I had no idea what I would be receiving! The sound of the cheering audience enabled me to overcome my paralyzing stage fright. This would be my eleven o'clock number in the show.

Leaping from out of the blue, the quarterback charged towards me like Jake LaMotta. Once again I was saved by Rodgers and Hammerstein. This time it was "Climb every mountain" that rang my bell. Planting my enormous torso stage left, I morphed myself into an immovable fortress, a statue ready to squash anyone in my path of destruction. I became Cyclone Karlotta! The naïve quarterback dove into my unflinching gigantic gut causing him to fall flat on his face and catapulting the pigskin fifty feet up in the air. The spotlight captured this unforgettable theatrical moment, following the ball's journey to the top of the ceiling until it miraculously plopped into my eagerly awaiting hands. What was I to do with it now? One of my supporting actors yelled, "Run, B., run!"

So I ran like Forrest Gump until it dawned upon me that I was headed in the wrong direction. The goal was towards the proscenium arch, not the rear mezzanine. With every ounce of stamina flowing in my being, I smashed through the line of actors and crossed the goal line. I had scored big time. The audience gave me a standing ovation while the director screamed at the top of his lungs, "That's the way to ***B***. *on the ball*!"

"White Squirrel Event Calendar"

Queen Karlotta & Princess Provincia's favorite childhood pastimes.

Memories…

JANUARY

Change sign at Burger Queen from 'Happy New Year' to 'Happy *YENTL*'. Barbra's classic masterpiece and directorial debut deserves to be a national gay holiday.

FEBRUARY

Prank calling. Order taxi and pizzas to despised Driver's Ed. instructors. Inform delivery peeps that resident is virtually deaf and to keep knocking and honking horn loudly and without ceasing. Secretly watch ruckus ensue.

MARCH

Cow tipping. Wait until dark. Sneak into dairy field and push cattle over before farm hands lose their bovine virginity. Suck teats. Run. Fast.

APRIL

Spring into camping season. Go to woods. Erect tent. Eat beans out of can. Burn leg trying to start fire. Frolic in poison oak. Freeze off ass. Get ticked off and catch Lyme disease. Get fishing hook stuck in left buttock. Avoid frisky drunken Uncle Donnie. Ponder ever going outside again. Why?

MAY

Play hide and seek in swanky Goosenobble section of town. Sneak into Cracklin's Chicken Factory and let loose 6,000 baby chicks who unintentionally wander next door into Vivian's Vinegar Vat. Scurry. Shhh!

JUNE

Frog gigging time. Equip oneself with flashlight, gunnie sack and a pitch fork like weapon called a gig. (Please google.) Head to nearest pond. Quietly walk around until bull frogs are spotted. Blind them with light. Stab frog in head with gig. Place in sack. Head home, cut off and fry legs. Become vegan for rest of life.

JULY

Take leftover 4th of July bottle rockets and insert them into barrel end of pellet gun. Aim and shoot lit rockets into unsuspecting nearby neighbors' houses with open windows. Let the fireworks begin.

AUGUST

Detasseling Corn season. Arrive at 4 am to ride in the back end of a plastic covered supersized wet pick up truck with pot smoking hoods and travel to corn city, Dekalb, Illinois. Walk endless miles in mud and 100 degree heat to pull out flowering tassels atop seven foot high stalks. Earn $1.82 an hour. Last one day. Awesome career launch.

SEPTEMBER

Clay City Fall Festival. Collect milk cartons. Cut out faces of cows to use as entrance fee. Eat all the desserts in cake walk game. Upchuck sweet treats into Persimmon Yangst's flowing auburn locks while riding the Tilt-a-Whirl.

OCTOBER

Vandalism month. Light brown bags of dog shit on fire. Ring door bell. Place a gallon of pancake syrup on creepy coworker's Chevrolet and cover with 16 bushels of leaves. Watch as he tries to find his newly created bush mobile. Sweet ride, dude.

NOVEMBER

Let's talk turkey. Change church sign from "St. Jude's Smorgasbord" to "St. Jude's Orgasm, now serving, 5-8 pm." Oh, come all ye thankful.

DECEMBER

Drive through Olney City Park's Winter Wonderland. Ride Rudolph and his 7 mentally disturbed twelve feet tall white squirrel reindeer. Find 16 nuts hidden in Santa's sleigh. Roast on open fire.

"White Ass in Whitewater"

The year is 1977. Our band instructor, Mr. Merl Merkin, informed us that our High School had been selected for the national competition at the University of Wisconsin in Whitewater. Screams of elation filled the cramped music room where we practiced for our weekly Friday night football half time performances. It was a rare opportunity for us to venture anywhere beyond our tiny White Squirrel nest.

Guess what instrument I got stuck in… I mean with? Yes, 'tis true, Karlotta the 300 pound portly poof, was allotted the dubious honor of playing the tuba. Or was it playing me? This sousaphone was extremely difficult to fit over my amply framed fortress of a body. My gal pal Provincia was playing a shiny new sterling coronet, an instrument resembling a trumpet but shorter and less brassy sounding, which oddly enough is a bit like Provincia herself.

Merl wasted no time in marshalling his battalion of bumbling hormone raging buffoons onto the field to drill us on a highly unique and meticulously rigid marching style. This new step in our routine was a cross between a Neo-Nazi Gestapo high stomping goose and a Celtic clogger conducting calisthenics on crack cocaine.

This movement was exhausting and not the easiest to execute properly especially for Karlotta and Provincia who were a wee uncoordinated, directionally dyslexic and more than a little light in our lavender loafers. We were continually criticized for being out of step, out of line and not yet out of the closet.

Our rehearsals were relentless. Finally, the big day dawned and we boarded buses for our trip to the cheese capital of America. Six hours later we arrived and went directly to the massive stadium for an extended period of rigorous practice. Our nerves and bodies were shot! How much more physical exertion could two nelly fifteen year olds endure?

In addition to the trophies and nationwide recognition, whichever school won first prize would be given the illustrious honor of being flown to New York City to participate in the annual Macy's Thanksgiving Day parade. The pressure was mounting and we were about to burst with excitement.

As the sun rose, we assembled, anxiously anticipating our entrance while watching our fierce competitors perform. Suddenly we heard a booming voice announce: "East Richland High School, take the field for competition!" This was it! With the down stroke from our drum major's baton, the brass section started the first stanza of 'Hava Nagila'. Everything was going swimmingly and the adoring crowds were clapping and cheering as they watched our frenetic feet galloping in perfect precision.

Now it was our time to shine in the tuba trio. The rifle and flag twirlers separated, signaling our grand entrance. Silence filled the dome. As I pushed down the valve to play my first note, I watched in horror as my gigantic white tuba bell began to wobble and soon came crashing down to the astroturf! I kept playing and marching in step as if nothing had happened, although I already knew that when something is mistakenly dropped onto the field, the school incurs a deduction from the total score. The rules also state the marcher is not allowed to pick up the discarded item as only an official can retrieve and return it. Do you think any judge is going to retrieve my big overblown bell and reattach it while I am goose-stepping to 'Hava Nagila'? *Oy vey is mir!*

Within mere seconds of the bell drop, another disaster struck. Provincia's belt buckle snapped, prompting his pinstriped pantaloons to plummet to the ground. On this particular morning, unbeknownst to anyone else, Provincia's bowels had also snapped, eliciting several episodes of intense 'sharting', which resulted in soiled fruit of his looming briefs. Thinking quickly, Provincia had replaced his ruined 'tightie whities' with a regulation baseball athletic supporter cup with fully exposed derrière. Provincia bent over to gather his trousers and simultaneously mooned Wisconsin. He immediately asked for assistance from first chair frumpet player, the neurotic Colleen Cooterpoof who was standing beside him. "Would you please hold my trumpet whilst I hoist up my pants?" Cooterpoof retorted, "That thing is too tiny to be a trumpet. It's a damn coronet!"

Provincia was flabbergasted as he glanced up to see himself in full close up on the Jumbotron with an audience of 30,000 fans pointing and laughing hysterically at his lily white butt cheeks. Sure enough, Provincia's posterior had been recorded for posterity! Another penalty imposed for exposure. Queen Karlotta and Princess Provincia had singlehandedly screwed any chance to win the National Marching Band competition and the coveted trip to New York.

We were the inevitable targets of blame, rejection and disdain. Our peers chanted, "You two prancing pansies are the reason we lost first place! Loser. Loser. Loser." All we wanted to do was return home to the safety of our white squirrel's nest and forget the horror of ever being a "White Ass in Whitewater!"

"The Great *GASP*ing!"

Let us travel back in time to review the beginning of my career as a naïve adolescent. Unless you had expert knowledge in White Squirrel reproductivity or desired to be a minimum wage earning burger flipper at a fast food franchise, finding work as a teenager was a formidable challenge. My friend Norma Nadine Noogan and I saw an advertisement for nursing assistants at the Chlamydian Convalescent Center, the preeminent elder care facility named after the popular perennial flower, not the unpopular sexually transmitted disease! The next morning we completed our applications and interview. We were hired instantly and told to report for duty at 7:00 a.m.

Day One: We met with the head nurse, Mrs. Hazel Horowitz, who discussed the various responsibilities and elaborated upon our detailed job description. In the medical profession we were referred to as nurse's aides, attendants and orderlies. To others we were known as 'Buttock Washing Bandits'! We were expected to assist in taking vital signs, bathing, grooming, shaving, dressing, walking, feeding, restraining, and collecting a myriad of specimens such as urine, feces and sputum. ***SPUTUM*** is defined in ***Wikipedia*** as 'the matter that is expectorated from the respiratory tract, such as mucus or phlegm, mixed with saliva, which can then be spat from the mouth.' Believe me, sputum was often spat but seldom collected.

Hazel began our tour. The center had three separate floors, wings A, B and C. The A wing was for people who could basically take care of themselves. B wing patients were completely incapacitated. Wing C patients had concurrent psychiatric diagnoses such as obsessive-compulsive disorder, senile dementia, exhibitionism, schizophrenia and Tourette's syndrome. Walking down the hallway, Norma whispered into my ear, "Let's run like hell from this cuckoo's nest!"

We had never imagined the things we were about to experience in this fully fledged mental maze of insanity. Our first patient, Fernie Fennel, was completely catatonic. Fernie was frozen in the middle of the floor, posing in a statuesque state as Venus De Milo. Suddenly, she came alive and began shouting in an endless loop of vocal spurts, "Nurse. Nurse. I need a nurse. I need to shit. Shit. Nurse. Nurse. Shit on the nurse! Nurse!"

Day Two: We met the adorable patient Bobbie Jo Bubbly who sprang into action by firmly tugging on Norma's right tittie. She spoke adamantly, "The milk in my breasts is frozen solid and I can't feed my baby. Help me feed baby!" Norma, still a tad shaken by her pinched nipple, reassured Bobbie Jo that everything would be fine. By the end of our second full day it felt like we had been working there for months as we were physically and emotionally exhausted after witnessing what would now be our new home.

Day Three: Norma and I were partnered on C wing. The first task of the day was waking the residents, showering and bringing them to the cafeteria for breakfast. Many had soiled their beds and needed cleaning as well as new bedding. As we approached the dining area, a coworker was feeding a gentleman named Forrest Fricker. All of a sudden Forrest jumped out of his seat and yelled, "Whooooooa Nellie! Stewball is loose! Corral that Shetland back to his stall!" Mr. Fricker had worked at a horse farm for 50 years and truly believed Stewball was galloping between the tables.

Day Four: There was never a dull moment in the Center. Walking down the corridor, we noticed what appeared to be little round meatballs on the floor. Had a patient spilled their lunch tray? Upon closer view, Norma Nadine examined the foreign objects then uttered, "Oh no!" Ms. Millie Mennurey in room B-52 who was known to have explosive bowel syndrome had spent the morning rolling her grenades of colonic cannonballs and was launching them from her room into the hall. Lovely. As we walked into Millie's suite, her right hand was solidly positioned by her head. She said endearingly, "Come here, Karlie. I've got a present for ya. I made it myself. I've been workin' on it all day!"

With that exclamation, Ms. Mennurey hurled one of her homemade cattle cookies, aiming directly at my rather large target of a head. I started to raise my hand to shield myself but the creamy butt nugget struck me in the face, popping out my right eye glass and coating my cornea with a shiny new covering. What a cow pattie mess!

Day Five: Hazel Horowitz summoned Norma and me into the nurse's station. She informed us that one of our favorite residents had passed away, Mrs. Ursula Underlay. We were visibly upset and soon discovered the limits of our nursing expertise. It was our responsibility to give Mrs. Underlay a sponge bath and dress her because the immediate family and Doctor were already on their way. We were frightened by the idea of seeing a dead body much less bathing and clothing a lifeless person, which really *raised* concern. As we entered the room, Norma and I were horrified by the sight and smell of this dear Soul. Her entire body was pale green and motionless.

Our hearts began to beat faster and we giggled to disguise our nervousness. Knowing we didn't have much time, Norma Nadine Noogan took charge and told me to calm down. "Let's just do this," she said quietly.

After carefully washing her body with a sponge, we started to dress Ursula by putting a fresh gown over her right shoulder. I gently placed my hands behind her head and at that precise moment, Mrs. Underlay's upper torso *rose up* from the bed and her mouth expelled a rush of air which sounded like a deep guttural cough! She fell back to her pillow. Ursula looked as if she was possessed and we were scared to death ourselves! Well, not quite death, but as Norma shrieked and screamed, I sharted my damn pants. We both ran as fast as we could down the hall and slammed open the emergency exit doors which sounded the alarms. The nurses quickly responded as they assumed a patient had eloped from the unit. Turning on the exterior flood lights, they saw us high tailing it across the nearest corn field!

Although Norma and I were completely freaked out by this incident, our love and compassion for the elderly brought us back to the nursing home. We were informed by several medical professionals that this last release or gasp of air from the body often happens to people when they pass, sometimes even after death. Over the next three years, Ms. Noogan and I had countless adventures at Chlamydian Convalescent Center but none as memorable as our own 'Great *GASP*ing!'

“*PEOPLE* who work my last Gay nerve!”

People who are the least qualified to birth, raise and nurture children having the most number of them.

People.... People who sing ‘*People*’ and other Barbra Streisand songs who *AREN’T* Barbra Streisand! I mean, *really?*

Riding ‘shotgun’ in a Dodge truck dangerously close to your Aunt Mayball whom, without solicitation, extemporaneously demonstrates her *explosive* bowel syndrome on the newly replaced cotton seats.

People who brag about how ‘Linked in’, ‘Facebooked’, ‘Myspaced’ and ‘Twittered’ they are but yet lack the ability to carry on a conversation in person. *Social networking my ass!*

Guys who advertise themselves as ‘Str8t’ on Craigslist in the ‘Men for Men’ section. Note to such: Real straight men are most likely to prefer genders *without* penises attached. Come out, come out wherever you are! (Also, please take the “GAY-Q” Exam.)

Sensing in your gut that you and your blind date are not compatible when he takes you to dinner at his favorite family style restaurant: *Pu Pu Shwot Pwot!*

Sitting by people in a movie theatre who speak more dialogue than the actors on the screen. I came to listen to *Meryl* dear, not to you and the tribulations of Cousin Frederna.

Social acquaintances who find it amusing to let their tiny tykes wander under our 8 top, 4 star restaurant table. Ooops, did I unintentionally kick sweet Sally again in the tushy. Gosh darn't!

Having your promiscuous paranoid schizophrenic second cousin who has *slept with Belgium* channel the Holy Ghost *by phone* to inform you of the need to repent of your rampant homosexual tendencies in order to avoid the inconvenience of eternal damnation. (Please see the chapter, "Wendy Warthole and the Holy Ghost".)

People who proudly proclaim their 'Pro-life' position except in the cases of War, Capital Punishment and *after* a child has actually left the womb.

Being frequently 'French kissed' by gregarious great Aunt Aggie during her peak Herpes Simplex II outbreak. It's the gift that just keeps on giving.

Having one's first sleepover as a burgeoning adolescent unwittingly begin at your sixth grade best friend's home whose open door 'let it all hang out' policy includes having no doors on the bathrooms and being subjected to Mr. Miltie's sixty year old sagging moon and Ms. Imogene's tumultuous titties perched atop the family laundry basket.

People who spend all day in front of an ATM. Read. Push. Insert. Collect. It's not brain surgery, sweetheart.

People who frequently comment to me on what a terrific father I would make and suggest I should try adoption or perhaps a surrogate mother, to which I respond, "I never want to own anything that I can't return to Bloomingdales with a receipt!"

Attending class reunions to be reunited with people you didn't like *the first time* around.

People who are so annoying that you are forced to take benzodiazepines on a regular basis to maintain sanity and avoid committing involuntary manslaughter.

Spending $5 on a psychic who informs me her vision of my future love life is crystal clear. Sadly, one of my exes however has put a curse on me and it will cost an additional $250 to have the universe remove it so I can be with my destined voluptuous wife. Why is it that psychics can *channel Zeus* but are apparently unable to see that I'm gay?

Dating someone whose pubic hair is the size of Forest Hills.

Walking into your old High School friend's home twenty years after graduation and discovering she has hoarded every single newspaper, magazine, scented candle, TV dinner, cereal box and sanitary pad since 1982. She is clearly stuck in the past and you are now stuck to her linoleum.

People who condemn drug addicts/alcoholics who are themselves nicotine rolling, caffeine tweaked, gambling the house, shop 'til you drop, carbohydrate intoxicated morbidly obese bigots!

People in their 40s who have 'consensual incestuous sex' with their relatives and then proceed to bitch, brag, blog and broadcast it to whoever will give them 15 minutes of attention. "Hi, the statute of limitations called. *Childhood ends at 18.* Just wanted to let you know. Thanks!"

People who wear thermal underwear tops and stained bulging sweat pants to work and who appoint themselves as fashion police to criticize your attire.

Being set up on a blind date only to discover that he has more hair on his sensory organs (nose, ears and tongue) than on his head.

Actors who long to sing and do so in the nonexistent key of S. ***S = STOP!***

Being swiftly served a tennis ball that lands a direct hit in your groin, cracking the family jewels and creating the emergence of a third testicle equipped with its own area code.

Walking behind a ripe relative who has a swarm of ferocious fruit flies desperately attempting to target and invade her wiggling anus.

Anyone who voted TWICE for Bush and Dick. You got exactly what you elected: The brain of a Bush and the soul of a Dick! *Great job, masses!*

Being shown a one bedroom apartment by its' current tenant, Ms. Betsy Ross (actual name), who begins the tour in the kitchen whose stove top ranges look like an Olympic playing field for *la cucarachas* who are bodaciously parading in and out of her moldy mac and cheese. The tour continues through the living room that she notes has a freshly painted ceiling which has also left saucer sized droplets of snow white blotches on every piece of salmon colored upholstered furnishings that were conveniently uncovered during the painting while stoned party. Finally, we arrive in the bathroom which seems fairly sanitary and normal until the shower curtain is partially drawn, revealing the back end of the porcelain tub which has been filled gingerly with ten inches of soil and grass covered sod and is apparently providing the abode with fresh dandelion and dill weed.

People on dating sites who misrepresent their current career as "CEO" of a mobile entertainment franchise only to subsequently find out later they travel 8 months a year as a Carny! How do you spell euphemism?

Being invited by an old college pal, Della Faye Frickasee, to spend a few days at her luxurious estate in Noxiousnille, North Dakota, and being directed to sleep on the floor in one of her spacious guest bedrooms on a 'blow it up yourself' air mattress NEXT to her freshly made queen size bed for fear that you might sweat and/or stain the bedding. "Dearest Della, Thank you so much for the considerate raft. I wasn't able to locate your pool. Sorry for the rather extensive mystery spot I left on your antique comforter that your ex-hubby told me was delicately hand stitched as a wedding gift by Gramma Gert. I feel so bad that I forgot to mention I'm a horrible somnabulator and one can never tell what nasty mess I'll get myself into or make in the bed. Much Aloha."

During the annual office "Secret Santa" gift exchange, being the ecstatic recipient of an unwrapped gray comb, used maroon coffee mug, and last year's bank calendar. *Tis the season to be chintzy!*

Having great great Aunty Bernice Wailuku regale you for the 178th time about her breast reduction procedure when she witnessed the surgeons dropping her nail like nipples on her knees.

HOMOPHOBES!

"YOU SAY GODIVA, I SAY *GO-DIVA*!"

The year is 1986 and 'tis Easter season in Squirrelville. The only difference is that in our hometown the bunnies are agile, aggressive and anorexic. They also climb trees and telephone poles with reckless abandon and store their nuts in holes. I was presently living in Manhattan and decided to make a surprise trip home to see my family. My dear friend Brad offered to pick me up at the closest airport, the urbane Evansville, Indiana. Only one year prior, I had moved to New York City with one suitcase, one thousand dollars and one huge dream to live the Big Apple life. I was happy to leave behind the corn fields and soybeans so I could stamp my own unique imprint in the famous concrete jungle.

The next day I was on my way to JFK for my flight to Chicago. While walking towards the gate, a Godiva boutique caught my eye. I spotted a gigantic gold oval $120 tin of assorted chocolates with pristine vellum wrapping. Wouldn't this be a wonderful gift for my mother?

My flight to O'Hare flew by and I was now waiting to board my connecting plane to Evansville. What a nightmare! Our luxurious jet looked as if it had just returned from its' third tour of duty in Sarajevo. I perused my interior surroundings and observed 6 passengers, 6 seats the size of sausage casings and a total of 6 biscupids. I, being 6 feet 4 inches tall, was selected for exit row duty, which in this petite air bus meant my ears would be strategically adjacent to the engine's mellifluous muffler, a diabolical chamber whose decibels registered high enough to qualify as an unofficial form of rendition used to interrogate suspected Al-Qaeda terrorists. My migraine subsided as we began to land.

I was feeling excited to be reunited with my loved ones. I assumed my beloved friend Brad would be waiting for me at baggage claim. Silly me. I searched everywhere in the tiny terminal but he was nowhere to be found. This was before the era of cell phones so I felt stranded. My parent's home was still 85 miles away. I placed my luggage by an empty row of seats and approached the counter to ask if this was the only place where people would assemble to await the arrival of their guests. He nodded so I returned to my seat only to find an old woman sitting in it.

She was wearing a charcoal gray skirt with matching jacket, pink cashmere sweater, mother of pearl necklace, brown knee high boots and a flattering fedora with a sky blue satin sashaying scarf tied around her hat. That crazy bitch had my golden tin of Godiva chocolates in her nimble hands and had ripped away the pristine plastic covering and had three of my expensive gourmet truffles hurled in her boca. I looked at her with utter disdain and said, "What the hell are you doing?" I was a livid New Yorker now and was about to call security.

At this moment, her little rosy rouged face looked up at me and I realized it was indeed my zany pal Brad in full drag regalia! I instantly fell to the floor in rotating convulsions of uncontrollable laughter, tears and snorts. This scene attracted a bit of attention from our fellow Hoosiers. Not only was Brad dressed as a woman, he had embodied the Dustin Hoffman female character 'Dorothy Michaels' and was speaking in perfect 'Tootsie' voice. After helping me stand up, Dorothy proceeded to ask a nearby innocent elderly man, "Oh my stars! What a remarkably handsome fellow. You are strangely reminiscent of my deceased fourth husband, George Gagoon. Would you mind taking a photo of my son and myself? His name is Karl. He lives in Manhattan, is quite successful and could buy and sell us both to Tangiers. Thank you very much." The poor doddery soul had not a clue that my senior citizen 'Mother Tootsie' was really a man in his twenties. After 'Dorothy' used the women's facilities, we walked to the parking lot and sped away. I asked, "Mother, where are we going and when are you changing your clothes and removing your pancake makeup and lipstick?" Still in character, Ms. Tootsie replied, "I am treating my son to a classy dinner and why on God's green Earth would I change this gorgeous ensemble? I am what I am!"

We arrive at this tacky wacky restaurant with dangling Chinese fans adorning the walls and ceilings. The décor style reeked of early 15th century Moo Goo Gone Bad. The waiter immediately approached 'Dorothy', giving her a hot towelette and inquired if she would like a cocktail. She answers, "Why yes, I'll have a strawberry daiquiri with lime twist. What a lovely blouse! Let's have lunch!" I felt like I had been kidnapped by La Cage Aux Folles!

After dinner, Dorothy/Tootsie/Mother/Brad stated they are too tired to drive the 90 minute trek to White Squirrel town. I was promised a 5 star hotel but instead was delivered to the doorstep of a Super 8. We checked into the motel as mother and child and checked out the following day as two men. Way to *go, diva!*

"How do you spell '*NILLER*' Please?"

Times were so tough that the economy was sagging faster than a nonagenarian's titties. I decided to be proactive and seize the day by moonlighting as the graveyard shift donut maker at Chuckie's Truck Stop in Effingham, Illinois, the glorious Crossroads of Opportunity. I fibbed a bit during the formal interview by stating I had managed a Krispy Kreme factory in Kankakee. Truth be told, I had successfully managed to devour two dozen of their glorious hot glazed wonders in one sitting. I got the job.

I came early to meet my trainer, Ernie Enyert, whose job was to teach me in twenty minutes how to proof, fry and frost a thousand donuts and their holes before the onslaught of famished truckers arrived at 5:00 am. Ernie spoke with heightened enthusiasm about his chosen career. "Your liquid lard is heated to 500 degrees. We only fry in top of the line Paula's peanut oil. Take your tongs and quickly drop two dozen durnits at a time into the boiling vat. If you have any questions, now's the chance to ask. Please call me Ern."

I spoke, "Ern, I can't help but notice a few burn marks on your hands. Some of them look pretty deep and discolored. Shouldn't you be wearing flame retardant protective gloves?" I thought to myself, "One burn Ern and I'm gone!"

Ern replied, "Son, I've been droppin' dough pert near twenty year and ever' onest in awhile you'll catch a fireball somewheres on ya."

"Why yes, Ern, I can see that." His hands reminded me of the Pyrenee mountain range in Northern Spain.

He continued. "Timing is everything in dough droppin'. You must flip 'em in the gurglin' grease at just the right moment. You have about a ten second winder. If you flip too soon, they'll be raw inside. Flip too late and they'll be burnt clean up. And whatever you do, make sure you don't puncture the durnits when you're turnin' 'em."

"Why not?" I asked naively. Who knew you needed an Engineering degree to make a damn cruller?

Ern retorted, "Because if the durnit gets stabbed by the tongs, it will become 'lead sogged' by getting pumped full of burlin' grease. That happened to one of our truckers. He bit into that sucker and within seconds developed a third lip! He's now known in town as 'triple lip Larry'."

I made a mental note to avoid wounding my delicate 'durnits'. Ern clocked out and left me to run the elegant dessert kitchen by myself. After 2 hours of proofing and preparing assorted frostings, it was time to put my elaborate training to the test. 1,000 donuts to go before my morning rush would ensue. How hard could it be? Drop and turn. Repeat. I put on my arm length industrial gloves which made me look like I was equipped to do battle with the four horsemen of the Apocalypse.

I dropped in a couple dozen and suddenly the peanut oil took on a life of its own and began popping everywhere so I spent most of my concentration avoiding 'catching a fireball'. As Ern would put it, I 'burnt clean up' the first hundred or so. My timing in tong twirling really sucked. The next batch was totally raw! I swear this was the deep fryer from Hell! I became increasingly frustrated and began displacing my rage onto the innocent pastries! I felt like Mrs. Lovett beating the shit out of her beloved pies. I was obsessed with getting at least one freaking tray of decent donuts to sell to my hungry truckers.

Three hours later I examined my finished product. 1/3 'burnt clean', 1/3 raw, 1/3 'lead sogged'. I was desperate. *What would Lucy do?* A wealth of sins and imperfections could be covered in frosting of course! I glazed, dolloped and pumped my long johns full of colored cream. Voila! Everything looked beautiful and perfectly arranged in my crystal clear display cases. I even impressed myself!

Most of my first customers were getting a dozen or so to go. This was a piece of cake. Finally, a sit down patron waltzes up to the counter and says, "Howdy, fine sir. I'd like a niller durnit?" I answered, "Excuse me. How do you spell '*niller*', please?" The gentleman in the cowboy hat the size of Ft. Worth continued. "Don't get smart with me, young feller. Do you know who I am? I am Mr. Chuckie!"

I gathered my wits and promptly served a fresh niller one. I knew I was playing Russian roulette with my delicacies. Please let my boss select one that is sweet, tasty and in the best possible shape.

Fate did not serve me or Mr. Moller well. With one bite, a geyser of grease erupted beneath the white cloud of powdered sugar, coating the owner with a Mt. St. Helen like experience. He did not appear to be pleased. His face could now be used as a tic-tac-toe board. He screamed, "You numbskull! You set my nose afire. Now git back there and make me a dozen of the best glazed durnits I've ever had or I'm gonna fire you flat!"

As I ran back into the kitchen, I accidentally knocked over a 25 gallon container of glaze. It flowed like an ocean of spermatozoa. Just at that moment, my supervisor, Helga Horbit, entered and slipped on the sticky substance, scooting her across the floor. I pulled her from beneath the fryer. She now looked like a 6 foot tall German cream horn. Helga barked, "Start mopping and clean up this mess! Don't stop 'til this floor shines like the face of the Sun."

I replied, "Helga. It's 8:02. I clocked out at 8:00. ***BYE***!" I ran as fast as I could and never looked back. And I never ate another 'Niller Durnit' again.

“Dating Disasters”

Before becoming a woman, Provincia actually used to date them. You've heard the classic proverb, “The road to Hell is paved with good intentions.” Well, Provincia hit that road hard and courted quite the motley crew of available females in White Squirrel town. From drag queens to thieves, hoarders, moochers and horse faces, Provincia's dating disasters left neither stone nor tittie untouched.

Pearl Skimmerhorn

Provincia's very first kiss and second base fondle was precious Pearl Skimmerhorn. Pearl's family lineage boasted a long line of hoarders, many of whom were rumored to be misplaced beneath mountains of Good Housekeepings and Quaker Oats in the master bath.

Provincia picked up Pearl in his recently wrecked Corolla. For some perplexing reason, two of his twelve year old cousins, Linette Kay and Matthew Jason, were also invited to share in the drive-in movie date festivities. Cuz Matt had just hit puberty and took merciless glee in tweaking and twisting until purple Ms. Skimmerhorn's newly sprouted nipples. ‘Net Kay’ kept busy dousing our bologna sandwiches with tabasco sauce and spiking Pearl's punch with cod liver oil and liquid laxatives. Just as Provincia dove in for his first tongue meets tongue exchange and boob squeeze, little Matthew adroitly dropped his drawers and shoved Pearl's nostrils squarely into his expanding sphincter just as he began to fire several launches of gas propelled emissions lovingly gleaned from his recent chili dog consumptions.

Ms. Skimmerhorn, being most unamused, slapped everyone's faces and telephoned her bull dyke sister Sonia who immediately rescued and sped away with Pearl on her Harley hog.

Hyacinth Haglet

Hyacinth Haglet was Provincia's first true love and Senior prom date. Hyacinth's physical appearance was distinctive. She had the cheeks of cherubs. They were also the circumference of continents. In fact, everything on Hyacinth was enormous, especially her bazooms. As a seventeen year old, her gazongas deeply captivated me. In addition, they could feed Finland. I copped my first feel in the back seat of Hyancinth's Honda. Unfortunately, her father Jervis was driving us home from a missionary convention in Teutopolis. Mr. Haglet peered in the rearview mirror and slammed the brakes, "What in the Sam hill is going on back there?"

Hyacinth retorted, "He's a milkin' me like Bessie the cow!"

I quickly repositioned myself and assumed my angelic stance. "I love your daughter sir and want to make her my wife as soon as we graduate High School."

Without missing a beat, mother Haglet chimed. "Take a

good look at me, Sonny, because this is what little Hyacinth is gonna flower into, give or take twenty years."

Given the reality that mother Haglet was a geographic destination unto herself, I heeded her admonition. We broke up the next day.

Fast forward ten years and many relationships later and the mysterious powers of the universe collided to reunite Provincia and Hyacinth once more. By this time, she had not only dated virtually every gay man in her area code but began to resemble a drag queen divette herself! Her closet was quite spacious and her vast beard kept everyone thoroughly covered. Hyacinth had become a successful toe nail polisher and local gossip queen. She made it her business to know everyone else's business. Ms. Haglet adhered to strict Victorian era rules of conduct when it came to sexual activity between us. There would be absolutely nothing below the boobs until honeymoon night.

On Easter eve, she was hospitalized for abdominal pain. Initially the examining physician suspected Hyacinth was in her 5th month of pregnancy. She quickly squashed that diagnosis. "Unless I have been unconsciously inseminated by amorous aliens or have become the world's second candidate for virgin birth, that ain't possible!"

As the boyfriend, I fully concurred. Nothing fun was happening under Hyacinth's belt. Finally, a sonogram revealed a benign mass the size of a firm California cabbage. The following week we met with her gynecologist. "Ms. Haglet has an extreme case of vaginismus."

"What the heck does that have to do with me?" I inquired.

"To be blunt, she can only comfortably handle a penis the size of a child's birthday candle or a miniature golf pencil." The doctor knowingly winked my way.

"Isn't that wonderful," I responded. We broke up the next day.

Melba Drood

Provincia's virginity was lost to the tempestuous vixen, Ms. Melba Drood. Her family was considered 'well off' as the owners of the county's sole glue factory. Melba's mug was a dead ringer for the retired stallion, Harry Hardonya, a favorite champion trotter of local horse lovers.

We met in Spanish class and decided to join 'El Espanol' club so we could attend an upcoming excursion to Spain. Passports in tow, we boarded our jet across the Atlantic. Since my roommate, Peter Poon, was dating Melba's roomie, Babette Baboonais, we swapped hotel suites, and our snooping adult chaperones were none the wiser.

This was the first time I ever saw the entirety of the female anatomy totally nude. What was a guy to do with all that interior plumbing? Sensing that Provincia was completely lost, Ms. Drood took matters into her own hands and led the way to coital bliss. Ever the temptress, she asked, "Do you want to look back in life and say you lost your virginity in Illinois or here in muy caliente Barcelona?"

Who could argue with the brilliance of that logic? It felt like it was over before it started. Melba, an avid chain smoker, blew into my ear. "So, how was your first time, big boy?"

Without thinking, I answered, "Kind of reminded me of making love to an ashtray."

Melba quipped, "Well then buddy, you have just smoked your last butt!" Touché.

Bagunyun Burl

Bagunyun Burl is known in the lexicon as the classic rebound girlfriend. She came between Melba and Verla. Bagunyun had a few minor idiosyncrasies. She had three chins, a face beaming with blackheads, a smashed in nose and an overwhelming fetish for chest hair. She also ate anything visible to the eye. My mother affectionately referred to her as a "narcissistic personality disorder who looked like a walking pepperoni pizza." All in all, Ms. Burl was quite the adorable gal.

Bagunyun was also the ultimate mooch. When I would take her to an 'all you can eat' restaurant, she'd eat all they had. At one point she stored a petite microwave in her hair. We were quickly banned as a couple from Billy Bob's Brunch Buffet. After Bagunyun demolished sixty chicken salad pastry puffs and half a wedding cake, mother resorted to padlocking the fridge on our date nights. Ms. Burl's appetite for men was equally voracious. Once she discovered Provincia's hairy chest, there was no stopping her man-eating mania. After devouring me whole, she left me high and dry in the lurch, dumping me for her next conquest, the burly Brent Buggerly.

Verla Pie

Verla Pie, doting daughter of Pot and Cherry, was a fascinating creature to behold. Verla seemed to meet all of Provincia's qualifications as the ideal girlfriend. She owned every Streisand/Midler/Carpenter album. She had seen every episode of "The Mary Tyler Moore show". Her dream vacation consisted of Broadway musicals, Sardis and The Plaza hotel. It was like I was dating myself in female form! Was this a dream come true? Slowly but surely, cracks began to form in our perfect relationship. I was in severe denial as I did not want to stop dating Mrs. Santa Clause. Verla was extremely generous. If I even casually mentioned that I liked something, it would magically appear the next day. She was like my personal genie with gargantuan breasts and size thirty six jeans.

Mother pointed out that Verla did have a few minor imperfections. First of all she noted that Ms. Pie wore black velvet constantly, even in sweltering August weather. Big deal, so she wasn't Ms. Fashionista. Second, the corner fast food joint noticed that each night Verla worked, their cash registers came up short $600. Purely coincidental to me. Besides, not everyone is a mathematical whiz in making proper change. Third, the Vincennes police were prosecuting a stolen watch from a downtown jewelry shoppe which happened to be the exact same model on my wrist.

Hmmm. Mother said I needed to confront Verla on her pathological lying and thievery.

I walked to Taco Tito where she was chopping buckets of yellow onions. "Verla, the cops were at my door saying my timepiece, my luggage and the designer clothes on my back are stolen merchandise. Is there anything you want to tell me, my darling love angel?"

Verla Pie refused to answer me and escaped through the back exit and was never heard from again. Mother knows best and I kept the goods. Verla *who*?

How the Elves stole "White Squirrel Christmas!"

Three naughty elves
on 24 December
made such a mess
that all would remember.

A crystal clear night
with freshly fallen snow
created quite a sight
and made their noses glow.

For this was "White Squirrel" town
decked in festive green and red;
but the elves were feeling down
and snuck out of their colorful bed.

It was time to get away
for a bit of holiday cheer;
so off to Fireside pub to play
and imbibe wine, liquor and beer.

A flame from long ago
who went by Bagunyun Burl
had bought new boobs to show
that she was such a big girl!

As Ms. Burl teased with laughter
flaunting her melons with ease;
The elves became mischievous after
way too many Long Island Iced Teas!

When Bagunyun's blouse popped right open,
eager hands were there for lots of gropin';
Her wardrobe malfunction led to slapped faces,
being bounced from the bar,
it was off to the races.

Driving through the Christmas park
made their hearts merry and gay;
but they found it such a lark
upon approaching St. Nick's sleigh.

How shocking to see Rudolph had been replaced
by a seven foot tall pink eyed white squirrel.
Such a display of tacky Yuletide taste
really pissed off the elves and made them HURL!

They rammed the car into its' head
going berserk, acting like a wino;
They smashed and thrashed until it seemed dead,
then tore the tail off the poor Albino!

"What the heck are we gonna do?",
said one crazed elf to the other;
"Don't you worry. Let me show you.
Now hand that tail to your brother!"

So across the town they began to roam,
taking the carcass of the critter they stole;
They dropped it in front of an old nursing home,
for it was time to return to the North Pole.

The disappearance of the rodent caper
remains a notorious scandal;
It made headlines in the White Squirrel paper
and they never caught Santa's little vandal!

"Isn't that Awful?"

Mary Jo Pro-*fessional* was born in the dustbowls of Wewoka, Oklahoma in the midst of the raging Depression. Although she was one of twelve siblings and slept three in a bed, she was unaware of her poverty status. Even as a young girl, Mary Jo Pro would imagine living in a big gorgeous three story home filled with beautiful furnishings and carefully selected works of art. She excelled in academics, graduating second in her High School class. She also went fishing for and successfully reeled in her smart Navy sailor man, a handsome Captain Jack of all trades.

In addition to raising three sons, working various jobs, directing choirs, being an avid gardener, participating in the Red Hats sorority, playing golf in the ladies' Country Club league and also singing professionally, Mary Jo Pro tenaciously pursued her childhood dream of becoming a successful interior designer. After finishing design school she began to teach decorating classes at the community college. Eventually she and her savvy business partner/husband purchased a historic Victorian home and opened a landmark high end retail furniture store that would emerge as destination shopping. Considering that the location of "House of Interiors" was in the middle of a tiny obscure town famous for albino squirrels, this was no small accomplishment indeed!

Being a wise and sophisticated woman, Mary Jo Pro was frequently sought for her witty and down to Earth advice to solve a myriad of life's problems. Her personality was one of a kind, part Southern Suzanne Sugarbaker, part sassy outspoken Karen Walker. She had a dynamic and unforgettable way of using four specific phrases in her inimitable words of wisdom. They are: "Isn't that awful?", "I feel so bad.", "S/he can't help it!", and the ubiquitous "Bless her heart."

Here are some snippets.

Ms. Helena Mowry, a 280 lb. female peer struggling to lose weight, was desperate for help. "Mary Jo Pro, I don't know what I'm doing wrong. I have counted calories, steadfastly gone to the gym and paid a fortune to be hypnotized to drop the fat. I've cut out sugar and trans fats plus I have added flax seed to my steel cut morning oats. I was kicked out of Weight Watchers, finished a month of Deal a Meals in three days and practically ate Jenny Craig herself. I'm at my wit's end, I tell you!"

Mary Jo Pro-*fessional* thought for a moment and answered simply, "Dearest Mrs. Mowry, how do I say this. You need to simply back up from the table. If it's on your lips, there go your hips and honey your hips have gone from here to Eternity."

She added, "Bless her heart. She's the size of Manitoba! Isn't that awful? She can't help it. I feel so bad!"

Another rather large gal pal, Miss Lulaball Limabean, reported having severe marital issues. "Mary Jo Pro, I'm beginning to think the romance is evaporating from my 40 year old marriage. I've tried new floral perfumes, sexy lingerie and scrumptious candle lit dinners along with his favorite Sinatra music. Nothing seems to work. What in tarnation am I doing wrong?"

"My sweet pea Lulaball, don't you think a minor makeover is in order? First, your belly is the size of a third trimester dingo. Whole Foods called and would like aisle six returned. Second, your hair hasn't been cut or styled since 1952 and the view from your back side resembles a mutated horsetail from a misguided High School production of Equus. Shall we schedule a salon appointment?"

"Oh my, isn't that awful? She can't help it. I feel so bad. Bless her heart!"

Another asked for a point of etiquette clarification. She explained, "I invested a great deal of creative thought into my mother-in-law's expensive Christmas present and was able to give her the perfect gift which she adored. Guess what I received from the affluent Mrs. Kora Carterette when I opened my package? A single sleeve of forest pine scented lye soaps from that cheap dollar store! I could feel the anger rising within me and both eyes rolling back into my head. I began to practice my anger management skills and counted to ten while taking deep diaphragmatic breaths. I used visualization techniques I learned from reading Deepak to let it all go by surrendering it to the universe for the highest good of all concerned. I felt free of my negative energy once and for all. I affirmed with a smile, "It's the thought that counts!"

Mary Jo Pro retorted, "Pine scented dollar store lye soaps. Are you kidding me? You're exactly right. It is the thought that counts. So what the heck was she thinking? Knock,

knock, anyone home? Isn't that awful? I feel so bad. She has the exquisite taste of a vagrant. It's time to take out the trash, precious Lynn. She can't help it. Bless her heart!"

With those four magical phrases, Mary Jo Pro-*fessional* happily dispensed sage advice to all who inquired. On an ironic twist of fate, it turned out the aforementioned mother-in-law had intentionally given those lovely smelling bathing goodies as a joke. The real gift was a $100 bill which was placed inside the card that the unamused recipient had angrily tossed into the fireplace unopened!

ISN'T THAT AWFUL?

“Provincia *Plunges!*”

What would possess a 35 year old man who lacks a sense of balance, direction and coordination to pay $400 to voluntarily jump out of a plane at 5,000 feet? I am still trying to understand that conundrum myself!

My therapist at the time, Dr. Doyle Diddler, thought some ‘in vivo’ therapy would cure me of my acrophobia. When I was a child I became severely afraid of heights after nearly falling from my parent’s roof. Since that time just merely standing on a small ladder or a table would make me feel woozy and send shivers up my spine.

Dr. Diddler advised, “All the Benzos on this planet are not going to heal the wounds of your childhood trauma. You have to look your phobia directly in the eye before you can kiss it goodbye forever!”

I queried my shrink. “So you’re saying in order to cure my fear of being in high places I need to jump out of a plane several thousand feet in the air?”

“That is precisely what the Dr. ordered.”

I registered for the Skydiving course in Cape Girardeau, Missouri, a rural town famous for lakes and Limbaugh. Perhaps I should have paid more attention to this omen. Since Doyle recommended I face my fear alone, I chose ‘going solo’ over the wildly popular ‘tandem’ jump where usually a husky and highly experienced skydiver is strapped behind you doing all the work so you can simply enjoy the ride while he is riding you. What the heck was I thinking? I spent the first hour of the day in Orientation class which consisted of watching a video tape of angry attorneys informing us in quite explicit terms that if we suffer an injury, sustain traumatic brain damage, go into a vegetative state or simply splatter to death on the ground that Stella's Skydiving Ranch cannot be held legally liable or be sued for any reason by us or any surviving relatives. This was comforting to hear.

Next we did 'simulated' jumping, landing and rolling off stacks of hay piled high in Bessie's barn. Then came chute pulling practice. It was refreshing to learn that our parachutes were pleasingly packed by volunteers at the local Welfare to Work/Get your G.E.D. Opportunity Center. Finally, our skilled air traffic controllers equipped us with minute earpieces in order to gently guide us to our bullseye target encircled on the land eons below.

I passed the written basic competency exam with flying colors and now it was time to see if I could actually fly. Six of us plus the pilot boarded an old defunct army plane which had been gutted. Up, up and away! There was no turning back.

"Geronimo!" yelled the first jumper. I watched intently as his descent into free fall mesmerized me. His arms were flapping away as if he were a 200 lb. bird gliding through the blue sky without a care in the world.

One after another until it was my turn. I breathed deeply, said a little prayer, and took the big heave ho! And so down and down I dropped. I punched the chute button and it suddenly hurled me back up. It felt like I had just received an industrial size wedgie by the wind! I noticed my chute's beautiful patchwork quilt design in an array of gorgeous rainbow colors. How fitting! As I looked below at my incredible panoramic view I had an instant epiphany! I was not afraid of heights after all. I WAS AFRAID OF FALLING! *Hello, therapist?*

Soon I began to hear voices. No, not inside my head, but in my earphones. I had forgotten about my professional crew assigned to strategically assist me in a flawless return to the ground.

"You're looking great," said my air coach. "We will guide you to a safe and soft touchdown."

I felt assured. Here I was conquering my greatest source of anxiety in the most dramatic way possible: SKYDIVING! The next voice I heard sounded like the muffled teacher from Charlie Brown. My fancy walky-talky was malfunctioning big time!

I heard, "Pwog Twogwaag Waff!"

I continued to float and fall. I couldn't see the humungous red target anywhere. The fast approaching landscape was not looking the least bit familiar to me. Was that river here before?

Coach Wing Dong Wang continued his futile attempt to reach me. "Waa hoddwab fwa wab wakk!" His tone sounded frantic!

The winds had picked up, blowing me way off course. I had to prepare for my landing. Now Wing Wang was yelling, "Pwog Twogwaag Waff!" Was he saying, "pull toggles left?"

I could see a small green hill below me so I took a leap of faith literally and grabbed both of my toggles, bringing them to center position. I immediately lost gravity and plummeted, smashing myself into the dirt, gingerly removing the cap from my right knee. Who knew that crab grass tasted like arugula filled sushi? Yes, I had forgotten to squat and roll.

The instructors darted over and drilled me like an oil well in Plano. "Why didn't you pay attention? We kept telling you to pull toggles left because you were headed for the lake and could drown. This ain't even our damn property!"

Why did I think I could navigate the sky when I flunked Driver's Ed. three times? I couldn't even roller skate much less do aerobatic somersaults in the air. Nevertheless, Provincia had summoned the guts to take the plunge and finally fired her shrink!

“Things that work my last Gay nerve: *ASSORTED NUTS!*”

Going shopping at Big Lots only to discover 900 townsfolk, 500 rednecks, 300 mullets and a grand total of 62 teeth.

Sitting in an aisle seat on an international flight next to someone whose bladder is the size of a frozen pea.

Religious zealots who try to sell me their point of view with no interest nor respect for my own. What happened to ‘do unto others?’

Politicians who toe tap, package gaze and play pocket pool in public restrooms and then feign ignorance and indignation about gay nonverbal ‘pick up’ code when they get caught. Please! Senator, you can Tom, Dick and Harry my ass!

Having more rolls on your stomach than Sara Lee has on the shelves.

Paying a small fortune to receive a ‘Lomi-lomi’ massage only to find yourself at the mercy of a 135lb. non-English speaking Japanese man who is skillfully using his elbows, knees and feet to contort your flabby body into a Caucasian salmon swimming upstream.

Furiously banging at the front door and loudly cursing your roommate who seemingly has you locked and chained out of your own apartment! Five minutes later, the door opens enough to allow a double barrel shotgun through it which is being pointed at your nose by its owner, a 78 year old shaky bells palsy Vietnamese immigrant. At this moment you realize you are one floor directly below your residence and suddenly sprint like a Kenyan marathon runner.

Green fanatics, rednecks, yellow teeth, orange carpet, blue foods, black and white thinkers, pink haters, brown snow and purple hair.

Accepting your best friend's dare to unwrap and consume all of your grocery items *before* check out.

Paying $995 for a day long metaphysical seminar in Sedona entitled, 'Mastering the secrets of success and happiness' only to go home with an autographed pamphlet, empty wallet, a magical mantra and a pair of miniature ruby red slippers to dangle from the car mirror. *Whoopee!*

Achieving 100% on your High School Driver's Ed. written exam only to flunk the 'behind the wheel' performance in 3 successive years because you unknowingly inserted the ignition key into the cigarette lighter, totaled the schools' 1972 Ford Pinto by smashing it head on into a parked garbage truck, sending Coach Leon Millspow into cardiac arrest. You eventually passed the class as the school ran out of teachers.

Being livid at the historical fact that IOWA legalized gay marriage *before* New York and California. Iowa, a state where bisexual means sleeping with *both* sheep and cattle. Good morning, America! Wake it up, progressive red eye bicoastals. You've been disgraced by *IOWA!*

Accidentally dropping 6 wads of thoroughly chewed Juicy Fruit gum into Cousin Nettie Kays' chestnut locks which sadly resulted in her scalp being shampooed with vinegar, peanut butter, and Aunt Jamima. After no avail, her head had to be shaved bald. Happily, she landed the male lead in the High School production of 'The King and I'. Years later this same relative would have her left nipple shot off in a freak Fourth of July incident. (Please see the chapter, "Tittie Tittie, Bang Bang!")

Sitting in an unassigned coach seat on MESSA airlines that is 1/2 the size of my overblown ass!

The Neanderthal 'Don't ask, don't tell' military policy. 'Hi, believe it or not, I can actually be gay and still shoot straight!' *Care to test my aim?*

Upon consumption of fourteen magic brownies, moving one's entire living room furnishings onto the roof on college graduation eve. Later being seen driving a sixteen wheeler semi truck through unsuspecting strangers' front yards and then tapping on their bedroom windows at three in the morning.

Being born 'directionally dyslexic' which means I was gifted with *one* constant sense of direction: ***WRONG!***

After weeks of emailing and texting, finally meeting your yet to be seen date at his scrumptious suburban home. After ringing the bell, he opens the door in full tuxedo attire and a toothsome smile from ear to ear. Glancing downward, you casually notice his fully erect six inch wonder which is also wearing a miniature satin top hat and red bow tied around the corona. Your date mentions that he rotates his member's wardrobe depending upon the occasion and has an assortment of tiny hearts, shamrocks, turkeys, wreaths and pumpkin heads. Happy holidays from dickattire.com.

Flying in a commuter plane from St. Louis to Chicago whose entire square footage is smaller than your kitchen.

When your family describes your dating repertoire as consisting of drag queens, hoarders, thieves, moochers and horse faces, the Universe might be trying to send you a message! (Please see the chapter, "Dating Disasters!")

To the entire profession of Dentistry: While all your other medical contemporaries are using the latest scientific cutting edge, state of the art, high tech, painless, patient centered laser gadgetry, you remain anesthetized in the Gunsmoke era with ear piercing power drills, wrenches, steel picks, brushes, floss strings and clove oil. What *century* are we in?

Seconds after jumping solo from an 8 seater gutted Army plane at 5,000 feet, you realize that your life long phobia of heights was erroneously diagnosed and that indeed you are actually terrified of falling! What color is your parachute, my dear? (Please see the chapter, "Provincia Plunges!")

Receiving a forwarded email which at the end demands, degrades and threatens to put a hex on you if you do not keep the chain going by sending it to a minimum of 10 more unsuspecting people. *EARTH to CYBERSPACE:*

Unless you pay me beaucoup $$$, you do NOT get to order me to send your idiotic emails to my entire address book!

While walking on 6th avenue, being tag teamed by PAID charity workers (oxymoron) to donate monthly payments on my credit card in order to save the rain forest, whales and their own underemployed temp. asses! Yes, I know it is your job to annoy and solicit me while I am innocently walking on the sidewalk and consequently it is my job to ignore you with utter disdain.

Being an excited 15 year old male member of a High School Marching band who is looking forward to winning the National Championship only to lose one's dignity, tuba and pants on the field in front of 30,000 laughing and pointing fans! (Please see the chapter, "White Ass in Whitewater!")

SMEGMA!

"HUMUHUMUKUNUNUKUAPUA'A"

You know you've entered into a spanking new culture when your capital city ends in "lulu" and the official name of your state fish is "Humuhumukununukuapua'a", which translates into 'fish with a pig's nose'. As a kid vacationing in Hawaii I wondered what it would be like to wake up in January to sunny skies and 78 degrees. I used to day-dream on my heated water bed and pretend I was floating in the crystal blue Pacific. After stagnating in a series of indistinguishable small Southern Illinois towns, I decided to save every cent and move 5,000 miles away to Oahu. Considering the fact that I didn't know a Soul there nor did I have any job prospects, this was a pretty ballsy move to a celebrated rock in the middle of the ocean.

The first thing I experienced when I stepped off the jet was a beautiful aroma of fresh tropical flowers that permeated the air. The second thing I noticed was how outrageously expensive my cab ride was from the Honolulu airport to my Waikiki beach hotel. What mess had I gotten myself into this time? Practically everyone thought I was insane to quit a secure position in the Midwest and risk it all for some Polynesian pipe dream. Nevertheless, I dropped all my naysayers flat and did what I wanted anyway. Alo-freakin-ha, baby!

I began searching for affordable apartments. An elderly Japanese woman named Beatrice Sasahuna offered me a one bedroom condo. She was generous, eccentric and had 14 cats that ruled the roost. It was kismet. Beatrice was a wealthy and shrewd business woman who also wielded a wonderfully wicked sense of humor. Not only did she care less how others perceived her, she would have great fun at the expense of their misperceptions. For example, she would intentionally dress in the shabbiest clothes she owned, leave her hair wildly unkempt and *then* go food shopping. Sometimes tourists would assume she was a homeless bag lady and insist upon paying her bill which usually included a case of tuna for her beloved felines.

She relished in her victory and would regale, "Look at dem dumb haoles. Dey tink I am poor yet I could buy and sell those nutty buggahs!"

I needed to go to the closest grocery store and stock up my fridge. Take about a rude awakening! Milk was $8.29 a gallon. Generic ice cream was $6 per quart. Forget about cheese. I instantly became lactose intolerant. After spending fifty bucks, I didn't even need a bag to carry everything I purchased. No wonder the natives grew their own damn food. Everything else had to be flown in. It dawned upon me that I was now living in tourist trap city. Visitors obviously didn't give a crap about the high cost of cereal or meat.

They were on vacation. Yes, I soon discovered this was indeed Paradise and you paid dearly for it through the nose and out the ass!

I also realized that people born in Hawaii spoke their own specific dialect and if I wanted to be accepted I would need to learn it quickly. 'Pidgin' is a unique local island language unto itself with a specific cadence, inflection and tone. It reminded me of Yiddish with a sing-song drop at the end of a sentence. One of my Samoan neighbors, Mr. Sulu Kaaawa, attempted to instruct me.

Sulu said, "Remember in Hawaii you speak every single vowel. So my last name is pronounced *'Ka-a-a-va'*. My middle name is *Ka-ne-ka-po-lei*." Oy vey. Vanna, may I buy a consonant please?

Time for some vocabulary basics.
How are you? = *"Howzit?"*
Do you want to fight? = *"Eh brah, you like go beef?"*
Do you want to smoke pot after work? = *"Eh, try pakalolo pau hana?"*
The food at the new café is awesome! = *"Buggah, da grind at da kine is brok da mout!"*

Pidgin was contagious and I was catching it.

I had decided to use mass transit over buying a car. Considering the fact that I flunked Driver's Ed. and I could see myself careening into the ocean, mountain or nearest volcano, I thought this was a prudent move. I boarded the express bus downtown for my job interview with the State government. I became extremely irritated as I had apparently sat next to someone whose bawling baby needed changing badly. I yelled at my stop, "Clean up that messy keiki's okole!"

This translated into "your baby's ass just stank up the whole friggin' bus!" I caught some 'stink eye' from the infant's mom.

As I entered the building, I reached inside my briefcase for my resume and was promptly pooped upon by an inopportune pidgeon passing overhead. I went into the nearest restroom to refresh before my group interview. To my surprise, I was still carrying with me the unmistakable odor of that brat's dirty diaper. Now I was livid! It was as if the toddler had shit directly on me without my knowledge. I glanced down and realized I had stepped in dog doo-doo and had blamed it on the baby. I almost went 'shi-shi' in my pants! After I cleaned myself up from the bird, canine and my own personal crap, I walked into the conference room and was greeted by seven of my potential coworkers and the boss, Curt Kukumokopakaulu. I was surrounded by a sea of Asians. Upon seeing me, the entire group broke into uproarious laughter. Did I still have animal droppings on my forehead or what?

Mr. Kukumokopakaulu explained, "Sorry, but we couldn't help but giggle because it is so apparent you are not from here. No one in the islands wears suits and ties. Loud golf shirts and flowery mumus is the norm. That being said, why should we hire someone who is not familiar with our customs or community?"

I responded, "Because I manage a residential building here and my tenants are Korean, Filipino, Tongan, Japanese, Chinese, Vietnamese, Taiwanese and hapa haoles out the wazoo. I have also learned my way around and know how to enunciate perfectly, 'Mele Kalikimaka, Nuuanu, Moiliili, Liliuokalani, Namahana, Kilauea, Humuhumukununukuapua'a, Mahalo Nui Loa!'" How do you like them pineapples?

The hiring committee laughed again but I got the job.

Much to the dismay of my initial doubting Thomases who latter begged to come vacation at my 26th floor condo, I stayed in Aloha land for another seven years. After that, I once again moved thousands of miles away to yet another remote island paradise: **MANHATTAN!** *And I'm still here.*

“You’re NOT in *Bangladesh* Anymore!”

Don’t get me wrong, I am a voracious lover of diversity. It has been said that New York City represents at least 182 countries with their accompanying languages and dialects. I don’t know who said that but odds are they didn’t say it in English. We have a uniquely bizarre situation happening in America. Something tells me if one immigrated to Lyon in France that after several months one would become fairly fluent in French, the nation’s sovereign language.

This is not always the case here in the welcoming Big Apple. I often meet people who have lived and survived in New York City for let’s say a *quarter century* and currently speak and comprehend approximately 8 words of our official tongue, which to my understanding at the last census was ENGLISH! Can we do the math? 25 years. 8 words. Help! May I kindly suggest legislation which mandates all ESL and LEP citizens be required to learn at least ONE new word per year of residency.

Last week I ordered my usual chicken chow mein from my favorite Chinese take out. However I received Singapore Ho Fun. As I did not desire to have the fiery concoction transform my mouth into a blistering towering inferno orifice, I attempted to communicate my dismay. “Excuse me. There’s been a slight mistake. This is not what I ordered. I asked for ‘chow mein’ not ‘ho fun’. This hot and spicy mess will burn me alive and contort my lips into tomato caprese. How may we rectify our dilemma?”

My sixty year old delivery person responded with the

sweetest and clueless smile. "Jess. Tank u, bose!" He then extended his right hand for gratuity.

Yesterday, the trains were delayed and I was running late for work, so I decided to do what normally only tourists do: hail a cab. Upon entering the back seat I was overwhelmed with an unidentifiable noxious odor. I looked around to see if anyone was missing a dead goat's carcass. I alerted my taxi driver. "Please take me to Bushwick, tout de suite!" Upon turning off his blue tooth, my driver answered, "me no spik Engwish, bose." I responded, "Jess. Tank u." 8 words indeed. Thrilling.

I propose an addendum to Lady Liberty's open armed invitation to the poor, tired and huddled masses.

Please learn to speak the language,
You're not in Bangladesh anymore!
Yes, it's time to learn proper English,
Saying 'dees', 'dat', 'mao', 'quock'
Will not raise your IQ score!

If you want to have some class,
Stop talking through your ass;
To open immigration's door,
Don't sound like crazy Szechuan whore;
If your diction seems like you're on crack,
I will deport you to Iraq;
So you'd better learn to speak the English language now!

"PILL POPPING PARADISE"

One Sunday afternoon, during my leisurely stroll down Second avenue, I began to notice a familiar pattern regarding Manhattan's changing corporate landscape. Every block contained either a major bank or a drugstore chain. I was bombarded by Chase, Capital One and Citibank. Oh look, here's CVS, Rite Aid and the ubiquitous Duane Reade. What the hell is going on? I mean how many financial institutions and pharmacies does one damn city need?

Then, as I was nearly mauled by a double decker baby buggy, the circumference of Botswana, it hit me! New York is unquestionably the most stressful, hypomanic, totally out of control, fear based, mace in your face, always in a race, no space, fast paced place to exist on the planet. The citizens of New York need all those banks to hold all the money it takes to pay for all the pharmaceuticals prescribed to cope with the madness that is Manhattan! This was pill popping paradise. If you don't like your mood, alter it. How does one cope with the city that never sleeps? You take a pill of course! Or two. Or sixteen! What is that song I hear in my head? It's the sound of anxiety, my dear...

Xanax and Valium,
Prozac and Codeine;
Klonopin, Demurol
Paxil and Morphine.
Lexapro, Ambien
Vicadin drip---
Please come along on my pharmacy trip.

Zoloft, Zyprexa
and fresh Oxycontin;
Ativan, Busbar
and Meth. before it's rotten;
Marinol, Seroquel
Percoset drip –
Isn't it time for a pill popping trip?

When there's no buck$,
and my job sucks,
when I'm turning blue;
That's when I go get my prescriptions filled.
Then I get the highs, but still yet I'm chilled
and then I don't feel so real!

Take the 'GAY-Q' EXAM

Have you ever secretly wondered if you might be gay? Well kids, wonder no more! Take Queen Karlotta's and Princess Provincia's fail proof 20 question GAY-Q Exam and score accordingly to see if you test positive for GAYDOM! Good luck and tell the truth, all you bitches and whores.

Please honestly answer each question "Yes" or "No". Score 5 points for each "Yes" answer. At the end of the Exam, total your points and refer to the corresponding analysis of your final tally!

YOU MIGHT BE GAY....

1. ...if upon initial approach, people mistake you for Lady Gaga. Yes ☐ No ☐
2. ...if you think the "Super Bowl" is a new culinary product line at Williams-Sonoma. Yes ☐ No ☐
3. ...if the positions 'pitcher' and 'catcher' conjure up something other than your favorite baseball team. Yes ☐ No ☐
4. ...if your impression of "Tootsie" is better than Dustin Hoffman's. "Oh my stars, that's a corn cob; let's have lunch!" Yes ☐ No ☐
5. ...if you named one of your pets Barbra, Bette, Cher or Tina. Yes ☐ No ☐
6. ...if you host parties for the Academy Awards. (Note: If you also host parties for the Tony 'Antoinette Perry' Awards, along with being gay, you are a flying nelly bottom queenette!) Yes ☐ No ☐
7. ...if you are obsessed with the Barefoot Contessa. We love you, Ina Pearl Sue East Hampton Marie! Yes ☐ No ☐

8. …if you frequently use the words, “hello”, “precious”, “newsflash”, “please”, “horrid”, “whatever” and “hot mess!” Yes ☐ No ☐
9. …if you’ve seen Barry Manilow in concert 15 times and you were not born with a vulva. Yes ☐ No ☐
10. …if your lifetime wish is for Liza to sing her mother’s songs…at the Palace. Yes ☐ No ☐
11. …if you own the entire series DVD set of “The Golden Girls” and “Designing Women” and yet continue to watch the reruns on Lifetime. Yes ☐ No ☐

    …Score 5 bonus points if you called in sick and flew to New York to attend Bea Arthur’s memorial service at the Majestic. Yes ☐ No ☐
12. …if you don’t know the names of your congressional representatives but you do know the names and cities of origin of every American Idol contestant. Yes ☐ No ☐
13. …if instead of saying the color “Green” you say “seafoam”, “sage”, “cactus”, “emerald” or “pickle”. Yes ☐ No ☐
14. …if you advertise yourself on “Craigs list” under “Casual Encounters” and refer to yourself as “straight”, “inexperienced”, “curious” and “vgl”. In addition to being gay, you are a malicious liar. Lovely. Yes ☐ No ☐
15. …if you wholeheartedly believe Hillary Rodham Clinton (and you use Rodham) would not only do a superior job in governing the United States in comparison to Barack, John, Sarah, George, Dick, Al, Bill & Jimmy but that she could handily rule the world as well! Yes ☐ No ☐
16. …if the task of ‘bleaching’ doesn’t refer to your hair or your laundry. Yes ☐ No ☐
17. …if you’ve had parts of your body sucked, tucked, plucked, sculpted, implanted, lasered, waxed and injected with toxins and butt fat. Yes ☐ No ☐
18. …if you are able to ‘take flight’ without the assistance of hydraulics or NASA. Yes ☐ No ☐
19. …if you are known in the community as a professional in ‘water sports’ and you’ve never actually been in a body of water. Yes ☐ No ☐

20. …if during your annual proctology examination, the Dr. appears alarmed upon the retrieval of gerbil treats and you are not a pet owner. Yes ☐ No ☐

SCORING KEY:

Add up your total score and refer below to the corresponding category:

00–20	You are a gay friendly, metrosexual leaning fag magnet/fag haglet
25-40	You are now entering the “All Pink Triangle Zone”!
45-60	You could play the lead in the screen version of “Liberace”!
65-80	You have slept with the island of Manhattan. Queens is not your borough destination. It is your DNA!
85-100	The Statue of Liberty has officially commissioned the use of your flame as auxiliary reserve illumination. Light it up, Mary!

"Wendy Warthole & the Holy Ghost"

I was blessed with this paranoid schizophrenic relative who shall remain nameless, Wendy Warthole, charming soul, who recently converted to a new religious sect: the All Saints Assembly of Damascus. Was this the same place where St. Paul with the tenacious thorn in his side was struck blind? I digress.

Apparently, a core belief is that one can and should receive the spiritual gift of 'speaking in tongues'. Sadly, I am not referring to the art of cunnilingus, which is another gift that rarely presents itself. 'Tongue speak' is the channeling of an other worldly entity intent upon delivering a divinely inspired message to a chosen recipient.

I decided to call Wendy as I had heard at a recent family gathering that times were tough and she was going through a rough snatch, so I thought I would perform a good deed and reach out to her with an open mind, kind heart and a listening ear. Lucky me.

The following is our dialogue, verbatim.

Wendy: "Hello?"

Me: "Hi, Wendy. It's your cousin. How are you, dear? We surely missed seeing you at the family reunion last month."

Wendy: "Child of the world, the next voice you are about to hear is not mine. It is that of the

Holy Ghost! Be ye prepared to receiveth thy message."

Me: "Wendy, is there someone else in the trailer with you, Love? Should I call 9-1-1?"

Cousin Wendy's voice suddenly and dramatically dropped 5 octaves and was now speaking in a distinctly darker tone. Think Sling Blade meets Bela Lugosi with a tinge of Ernest Angley.

Wendy as The Holy Ghost: "Son of Cartier, you have sinned and come horribly short of the kingdom and the power and the glory of Almighty God, hallowed be thy name, on Earth as it is above."

Me: "Well, thank you, sweet precious darling spirit. What a lovely way to say hello and welcome to town. Why yes, Wendy, we have all sinned, haven't we, angel of mine? Some of us have actually slept with the father, son and Holy Ghost!"

Wendy as The Holy Ghost: "Thou hast fornicated, adulterated and subjugated thyself as a homosexual. Thou has especially committed the mortal sins of heinous anus and Leviticus."

Me: "Wendy, does Mr. Ghost have a name? Please let him know that we've been using the term gay now for nigh onto forty year. Wouldn't want Damascus to be out of touch?"

Wendy as Holy Ghost: "Thou has been disrespectful to the Holy Ghost. You must repent because you're bent! You are hereby condemned to the flaming gates of eternal hell and damnation."

The Ghost now begins to sing in monotone and is brutally flat. "Condemned forever and ever and ever and ever. Amen!"

Me: "Wendy, I don't quite know how to respond to that. I'm happy you taught your pet ghost to sing, albeit in the seldom heard key of Q. I so appreciate the nonjudgmental Christ like sermon as revealed in the gospel of Warthole. As for condemnation, you are absolutely spot on, honey! I am a fornicating, bent with a dent, flaming ball of queerdom, precious, and I love myself and so should you! Also, I forgot to mention that I have a ghost with me as well and her name is Gomorrah Gay Goo who occasionally moonlights at Minskys as a transgendered drag queen. Ghost Goo has a message for you."

Ghost Goo: "Wendy Warthole,
even though you've been a cheesy ho,
and have slept with Harry, Mary and Moe,
with zero tolerance to show;
It's time to stop and think,
although I'm colored pink,
my heart is sweet and true
and still has love for you! ***Good Night!!***"

“*WORKING* Works my last Gay Nerve!”

Working for a boss whose IQ and BMI scores are identical.

While working as a waiter at a well known Italian establishment in NYC, I was walking up a flight of stairs carrying a massive tray of food with a variety of dinner entrees. Just as I reached the 8th step, a rotund Welsh woman brushed by me causing me to lose footing. At that moment, a plate of pasta Bolognese lifted from my wrist and *took flight*, solidly landing atop a bemused customer’s head, coating her stiffened coiffure with a new steaming layer of angel hair al dente and bouncing a lone extra large meatball off her nose.

Having a 400 lb. psychotic patient hurl an entire urine soaked sofa at your nose. (Please see the chapter, “Can we say, Psych. Ward?”)

Working the graveyard shift and being assigned the task of proofing, frying and frosting 1,000 donuts. Five minutes prior to the end of your shift, you *accidentally* spill a 25 gallon container of glaze, flooding the entire restaurant and sailing your supervisor Helga Horbit beneath the stove. (please see the chapter, “How do you spell *Niller*, please?”)

Following my recent promotion, I offered my services as a volunteer somalier to a fellow waitress who was inexperienced in the art of opening champagne. As I removed the aluminum wrapping and wine casing, my thumb slipped, rocketing the cork to the ceiling, ricocheting and softly popping a boisterous toddler in the forehead.

While working at Burger Queen, being assigned the glorious task of rejuvenation, a jovial job which consists of using a hose to squirt liquid grease, which is set at the temperature of Hell, into gigantic vats that fry spuds and nuggets. At one point, the hose gets away from you and fries your right toe instead of the taters.

Retail shop assistants in luxury designer boutiques who treat you like low life vermin infested trailer trash that have no money to spend. Prima Donna, you work for minimum slave wage and it is your job to kiss my consumer ass.

Having such a lousy job you wish you could trade it for what's behind door #2.

While working at the White Squirrel Holiday Mart you announce tonight's entrée specials as 'meatloaf, fried chicken, baked lasagna and fresh Norwegian cock...*COD!*'

On your 3rd day of work, having your 77 year old non-English speaking Romanian supervisor, Marbella Burka-Sinduza, accuse you of sexual harassment by attempting to unleash her bra strap and commit frottage against her left thigh.

Getting a work email while vacationing in San Paulo, Brazil, informing you that one of your retail staff has 1) shit his pantaloons, 2) wrapped said soiled trousers in a jumbo garbage bag and 3) hand delivered them to show your corporate colleague. Note: This person is the size of *Darfur* and coincidentally also has severe hydration issues!

While working in retail, having a customer approach and ask, 'how the hell do I get out of here' to which you quickly retort, 'how the hell did you *get in*?'

Announcing tonight's dinner specials as a 'delicious pan seared venison in a red wine reduction served with placenta...*I mean polenta*!'

Working with a Paramahansa Yogananda wannabe who at a recent unscheduled encounter outside a public elevator proceeded to hold conversation with the company's CEO while bent over, *chin to shin*, with her head swinging to and from between her ankles. This is apparently known as the 'downward facing crazy dog swinging up my own ass' position.

While cofacilitating an 18 member all male batterer's anti-violence feminist group, you begin to nervously rock back and forth on your metal folding chair. After losing balance and nearly falling off the seat, you grab what you presume is the back of the chair next to you, steadying your grip, pulling yourself up, only to be greeted with the surprising gasp of your sole female coworker, Doralee Donilly, whose gel filled left tittie you unwittingly grabbed, twisted and tweaked to hoist yourself up from the floor. Afterwards Ms. Donilly responds, *"Hello?"* You state, "Well it was harder than the Rock of Gibraltar!"

While working as a Maitre'd in an acclaimed fine dining brasserie, people who approach asking if this is indeed a restaurant to which you respond, “No, my dear, it’s a hair salon. *Would you like a perm?*”

While working at Chlamydian Convalescent Center as a male nursing assistant, you are the lucky recipient of a baseball sized turd affectionately lobbed into your face, adhering to and busting out your eye glasses. Just call me Cyclops in the morning. (Please see the chapter, “The Great *GASP*ing!”)

While attaching parking tickets to windshields as the only male meter maid in Charleston, Illinois, I was routinely pelted in various body parts with rotten eggs and garden ripe tomatoes. *Tossed salad, anyone?*

On week two at your new job at a private urban college, you casually notice a media crew outside the Admissions building. Minutes later, you observe three of your new colleagues being forcibly hauled out in handcuffs and shackles. Later, on the evening news, it is reported that staff had been caught printing and selling falsified degrees to students without that pesky accreditation requirement of attending classes and taking competency examinations. *Today we have a $199 sale on Juris Doctorates!*

SPAM/SCAM!

"DISHING with *DELENE!*"

Q: Ms. Delene Piñata, how would you describe and introduce yourself?

A: Hello. My name is Delene Piñata. I am a 72 year old vibrant sexually hyperactive single progressive Upper West Side interior designer extraordinaire thrice widowed heiress. My greatest strength is that I say exactly what I think without censure. I speak the truth as I see it. My bubble thoughts and my words are one and the same. My most unique quality is my speaking voice which sounds quite a bit like Minnie Mouse on an espresso I.V. drip. The more I talk, the faster I speak until I morph myself into a shrieking squawking chicken. You've heard of bird flu? I have bird tourettes.

Q: Ms. Piñata, are you worried about Global Warming and the gradual erosion of the O-Zone?

A: Now why in the world would I worry about it? I created the dern thing. Global Warming is the best damn paradigm shift that has ever happened to our solar system. What frigid mess couldn't benefit from a daily dose of some good ole fashioned gentle genital warming? Rise up and feel the heat, baby! Would you rather your tired corpse acting body be in Antarctica or Rio de Janiero? Warm it up, Willie! As for the O-Zone, thank heavens we are finally invading it and depleting that sucker! Do you have any idea how long my O-Zone and polar capillaries went unmelted by humankind? It's a travesty I tell you. I teach women classes on how to defrost, deplete and demystify their own O-Zones. The G-spot is so last century. O-Zone is de rigueur and the hottest place to be on Earth. Just ask the grand Miss O herself. It's just one big old melting party!

Q: There are rumors circulating out there about your sexuality. Would you describe yourself as primarily heterosexual, homosexual, bisexual, transsexual or perhaps even asexual?

A: Well, first of all whoever is starting these insidious rumors is showing their ass of ignorance to the world and apparently never showed that ass to me or they would know the absolute truth about my sexuality. My sexual orientation is "Trysexual", which basically means I belong and support every sexual category. If it's in Kinsey's research, believe you me I have done it at least once. I heartily endorse "Trysexuality". Give it a try; see if it is a good fit for you. If it's not your best pot of brewed tea, then maybe you are not meant to be a tea bagger, so then get yourself some hot chocolate or a hot toddy or better yet a hot South American and stay out of everyone else's bedroom. Why can't people stand in their own repressed sexuality business long enough to stay out of mine?

Q: Who is your role model in life and why?

A: Her name is Empress Adeline. Her motto is: "When I am stressed and feel like Hell, I go to town and SHUT DOWN CHANEL!" & "There's no need to sit and sulk for Adeline gets those IN BULK!" I adore her because she does not let what others think stop her from being true to herself and she knows how to get what she wants... IN

BULK no less! I call her my Empress Adeline as she rules the empire of the Big Apple like a beautiful Lioness. She defines FIERCENESS itself!

Q: What are your thoughts on the current Economic Stimulus package?

A: We have been in a serious downturn for a long time. Some call it an annoying recession while other experts say we are in a deep depression and just don't have the cajones to admit it. The reality is we are in a blistering hot crazy MESS of Stress! The best possible course of action is a massive Economic Stimulus Package. No amount is too big! Everyone needs to take a long hard look at their own package and start stimulating it slowly, then faster, faster, faster! Remember, real charity begins at home! Start loving and appreciating your own economy first and then spread it and keep on spreadin' it one by one until the entire country has been stimulated into prosperity for all!

Q: You seem to have a lot of creative yet common sense based solutions. Would you ever consider running for President Piñata?

A: Hello? Have you completely lost your entire moronic mind? People today would NEVER elect an old tough hugely titted strumpet like me who fearlessly speaks her mind and could not care LESS about trying to please the ever vacillating pollsters. Besides I am way too avant garde for ultra conservative, pro-violence but anti-sex in movies, still outraged over a silly exposed nipple on TV, afraid to let gay people marry and adopt children, USA voting majority! Honey, they want Queen Victoria to rule, not Queen

Delene! The day someone like me gets elected will be the end of civilization as we know it!

Q: Ms. Piñata, what is your relationship to money? How do you feel about the old expression, "money can't bring you happiness?"

A: That literally makes me want to puke! Let me tell you something. People who say that tired ass bullshit are either poor, pathological liars or psychotic! If you are poor, how would you know if money would make you happy or not? Does living in filthy substandard housing projects with roaches and rats bring you happiness? PLEASE, wake up people! If you are clinically crazy, then you are excused. People who are wealthy and say that money has not brought them some degree of happiness are the same people who claim they don't masturbate. They are ludicrous LIARS! Wake up and smell the CA$H! If you are rich and are NOT happy, then you should be forced to forfeit your wealth and give it to someone else who VALUES it and who realizes the truth that money gives you freedom and choices that poverty NEVER offers! GET REAL and keep it that way!

Q: Ms. Delene, do you have any parting words of wisdom for your readers, perhaps some life lessons you can share to inspire us?

A: Certainly! This is Piñata's Personal Philosophy in a pastry shell! Love and accept yourself exactly as you are now! Live the truth of who you are because nobody else can do you like you can! As much as humanly possible only do what you really desire to do. Forget about trying to please others and being liked by everybody. Don't worship stars. Be ONE yourself! Stop judging and start appreciating. Billions of people would give anything to have your life, so cherish and celebrate the GIFT of YOU every moment! Laugh, sing and say THANK YOU as much as possible! *GOODBYE!*

"TITTIE TITTIE, BANG BANG!!"

'Twas the Fourth of July
and we all came together;
Under a moonlight sky,
it was near perfect weather.

Lined in red, white and blue
there were tables of food;
Beer and wine flowed too,
ensuring all a good mood.

This was our annual swaree`
in dear Mama Kaye's backyard;
Friends came from faraway
to eat, drink and party hard.

A celebration to ensue
on this Independence Day;
Fireworks and barbeque
with surprises on the way.

As the last piece of cake and pie
settled deeply in our guts,
we turned our eyes to the sky,
sitting comfy on our butts.

We relaxed in the lawn chairs,
wiggling our toes in the grass.
We drank away all our cares,
having gained 10 pounds in our ass.

After the sun had set
with twinkling stars up above,
this would be the best show yet,
the rocket's red glare that we love!

A trunk load of fire power
Allisa bought for us this night;
to give us a meteor shower,
a colorful, spectacular sight.

Luis launched one after another
in beautiful spurts of green and red;
"Ay, caramba!" shouted my mother,
"Don't let that thing land on my head!"

Suddenly, as if out of the blue
a rocket misfired, striking a pole;
it ricocheted and split in two,
careening faster and faster towards its goal.

Sitting by Karl in the front row
was my ample bosomed cousin Linette;
who knew she'd be part of the show,
a happening that we'd never forget.

The fireworks hurled right into her chest.
"My tittie's on fire!" she yelled in my ear.
I looked to see sparks spouting from her breast;
a red hot cinder caused her nipple to sear!

She doused her boobs and ran into Kaye's kitchen.
Karl rushed to my side, not knowing what to say.
From inside the house, we heard
dear cuz just a bitchin'.
We laughed 'til we peed on this
"Tittie Tittie, Bang Bang" Day!

ACROSS

2. Princess Provincia's mother's initials?

6. Dorothy ate Karlotta's Godiva at this airport?

8. When you are Gay and free you are what?

9. Provincia's coronet made this noise?

10. White squirrels can climb these but Easter bunnies can't?

14. You may have Klienfelter's syndrome with this triple chromosome?

15. Mama Kaye adopted Tyrene_______?

17. White squirrel scientific name?

19. You may be "Nellie" if you take this test?

DOWN

1. Don't tease Provincia or Karlotta or this may come along?

3. These fell down in White Ass, Wisconsin?

4. This caught fire and was cindered?

5. You can marry your family member here too?

7. Olney's mascot?

11. It's a gay man's world?

12. We hide these as well but love when they are exposed?

13. It was her barbeque that we had a "Tittie Tittie, Bang Bang"?

16. Dundas got on one knee and gave this to Mindy Mae Mullet?

18. What Karl needed in 8th grade? (Initials)

WHITE SQUIRREL SCRAMBLE

1. 2. 3. 4. 5. 6. 7. 8. 9. 10. 11. 12. 13. 14. 15. 16. 17. 18. 19.

WHITE SQUIRREL SCRAMBLE

DID ALL YOU SQUIRRELS GET THE RIGHT ANSWERS?

S			M.	J.	P.				
H		P				T			K
E	V	A	N	S	V	I	L	L	E
R		N		Q		T			N
O	U	T		U		T	O	O	T
		S		I		I			U
			T	R	E	E	S		C
N				R			E		K
U		M		E			X	X	Y
T	R	A	I	L	E	R			
S		M				I			
		A	L	B	I	N	O		
						G	A	Y	Q

"QUEEN KARLOTTA's & PRINCESS PROVINCIA's 50 FAVORITE PHRASES!"

1. "SHUT IT DOWN!"
2. "I SMELL A MESS!"
3. "RAISE IT UP!"
4. "Bore, Bore, Bore, Chelsea."
5. "Husker-Du!"
6. "My name is Karl but you can call me TONIGHT!"
7. "I LOVE MYSELF!"
8. "How-do?"
9. "BYE!"
10. Any form of the word "HURL!" (Hurl it! Hurled! Hurl it up! Hurling! Hurlynna!)
11. "I swear to Goat!"
12. "NEXT!"
13. "Reach for the Stars, precious!"
14. "Walk with me, Be Popular!"
15. "LIEBCHEN! Pop the head. Smack the face!"
16. "You're done!" "I'm done!" "S/he's done!"
17. "Have you met me?"
18. "GOOD NIGHT!"
19. "WATCH ME!"
20. "She's Fierce!"
21. "I get those ***in BULK***!" (We love you, Ms. Addie!)
22. "Hi Dorothy Lynn Sue Kaye Marie Pearl June!"
23. "I can't be bothered with that mess!"
24. "I'm going to drop her/him flat!"
25. "I never met a pill I didn't like!"
26. "Cheater, Cheater, Compulsive Eater!"

27. “Shut your hole; mine’s makin’ money!”
28. “Choose your friends wisely!”
29. “I’m gonna kick you in the pussy and take all your money!”
30. “For those who have teeth, we have apples!”
31. “LICK ME!”
32. “CLEAR!” (Said loudly to masses of tourists in Times Square)
33. “And which dwarf are you?”
34. “I’m 3 with nature. There’s me, nature, and a Four Seasons Hotel Deluxe Suite overlooking it!”
35. “1968 called. They’d like their wardrobe back!”
36. “Friends don’t let friends live in Brooklyn!”
37. “Quelle surprise!”
38. “Dolores Dawn Deene got her hot twat caught in the toilette in Detroit!”
39. “S/he is dead to me!”
40. “The role of the Drama Queen is now being played by…”
41. “Save the song and dance for Broadway, Bitch!”
42. “Look, they took a varmint and taught it to speak!”
43. “Blow it out your BUUIITTT!”
44. “God created the world in 6 days. Mary Jo Pro financed it!”
45. “Hot mess on line 6. Hot mess on line 6!”
46. “Can we say, Psych. Ward?”
47. “Don’t go hungry; eat my hole!”
48. “My favorite word in the English language: COMP!”
49. “I’ve slept with Asia... well just ½ of it!”
50. “You have just worked my last gay nerve!”

"Get *OUT!*"

Are you sick and tired of being in the closet? If you answered yes then 'you have just worked our last gay nerve!', so 'SHUT IT DOWN!', 'RAISE IT UP!', and 'Reach for the Stars, precious!' Join us in the jolly gay world of excitement and 'Husker-du!' We want to take you *OUT* of the claustrophobic confinement of your wretched mismatched wardrobe. Let us introduce ourselves, 'My name is Karl but you can call me TONIGHT!' My sister from another mister, Ms. Provincia, notoriously renowned as the rice princess of Nolita, has a couple choice quips of her own. 'I've slept with Asia ... well just ½ of it' and 'if we fought a war with ya, I wanna whore with ya!'

We lived a long time in the sequestered seclusion of insecurity and let us tell you that flinging open the locked doors to fairy freedom is the ultimate liberation. So 'save the song and dance for Broadway, bitch!' and 'walk with us, be popular!' Life is too damn short to live a lie, hide and stuff your feelings anymore! 'Bore, bore, bore, Chelsea!' 'We smell a MESS!' So when that glorious emancipation day comes and you've finally had enough of heterosexual enslavement and you summon the chutzpah to 'Hurl it *OUT*!', then please refer to these empowering phrases to ward off your taunting tormentors. 'I can't be bothered with that MESS!', 'I'm going to drop him/her flat!', 'Shut your hole, mine's makin' money!', 'Blow it out your BUUIITTT!', 'Lick me', and 'NEXT!'

Your newly gay mantra each day is to say, '***I LOVE MYSELF***!' for only then will happiness embrace and envelop you from within! Delay no more for now is the time to open those flaming French doors, 'Ms. Dorothy Laura Lynn Kyrene Merrie Heather Anita Sue Paula Stacey Sunny Erin Kaye Anesha Stephanie Marie Pearl Adeline June!', and always remember to 'choose your friends wisely!' When in doubt simply say, 'Have you met me?', 'How do?', 'I'm gay and I'm FIERCE!', and 'I get those in BULK!' 'GOOD NIGHT!'

"Can we say, *PSYCH. Ward*?"

Once upon a time while nesting in the southern comforts of my small town roots, it became my deepest passion to grow up and move far, far away to the mysterious and enchanted land called Brooklyn. I adored boroughs for that is what rodents do best: they burrow from one borough to another! After all, I originated from the most famous rodent city in the country.

I was ecstatic to land my first NYC job in Bushwick. I had read that it was an 'up and coming' neighborhood in Brooklyn. After I gave Bushwick my once over, I telephoned the author of that particular article to ask for a clarification of terms. 'Up and coming' in comparison to what? *KABUL?* Had he actually seen the neighborhood... *IN THE DAYLIGHT?* As I ventured for a stroll, I was surrounded by boisterous bodegas, breaking the sound barrier elevated JMZ trains, gang graffiti, Christmas decorations hung year round on Throop street, shot out store fronts, and check cashing stores on every corner. Excuse me, but what happened to bank accounts? The thrill of the hip factor was totally lost on me.

The first day of my first job in New York City began with a tour of my new home away from home. As I had only seen Psych. Wards in movies, I didn't truly know what to expect. I would soon have my eyes opened wide! My position was officially titled "Psychotherapist", with myself providing the therapist part, not the psycho. As I was led down the locked unit halls, my heart filled with compassion. Like the old saying goes, "but for the spin of the genetic wheel, there go I." Perhaps with enough empathy and creativity, I could indeed make a positive impact on their lives.

While the charge nurse, Ms. Fontella Laduey, was introducing me to staff, a robust and delusional client, Mrs. Louise Limpopo, made a mad dash for my torso and began to briskly grope and fondle me like she was attempting to devour a vodka soaked Kielbasa.

She spoke excitedly, "You me husband. I meese you. I vant to schtupp you. Keese me."

Two Psych. Techs. ran to my aide and giggled. "Don't feel too special. Limpopo tried to schtupp a sunflower stalk on the terrace yesterday. Keese me!"

I readjusted myself and asked Nurse Laduey, "What is the proper protocol should a patient once again attempt to violate my personal space?"

"Get your keys out and haul ass," she retorted.

Good to know. After lunch it was time for me to conduct an individual clinical assessment. Her name was Erma Junkinette. She looked like two swizzle sticks with a blonde head attached.

"Nice to meet you, Ms. Junkinette. I must say you are incredibly thin. Are you currently dieting?"

"No, I have never been on a diet nor do I have a weight issue. I go for days at a time and literally forget to eat. It simply slips my mind. I don't know what hunger pangs feel like. Has that ever happened to you? I hear forgetting to eat is quite common nowadays."

I reviewed my entire short and long term memory history. I had forgotten my keys, my cell phone, my wallet, my watch, my clothes, shoes, name, date of birth, address, my race, religion and gender identity but I had never ONCE forgotten to eat!

The rest of the week I had up close and personal encounters with schizoaffectives and schizophrenics, bipolar ones, twos and rapid cyclers. I did recovery groups with narcissists, antisocials and borderlines. I had successfully dodged paint brushes in the Art room being hurled at my head and nearly missed the pleasure of having a urine scented royal blue pleather sofa land on my lap in the day room. I swear I had met every Axis 2 personality disorder in the DSM and that was just the staff.

After a few weeks I gained confidence in my therapeutic interventions and became strangely comfortable with the daily routine of an inner city mental hospital. I would begin each day leading a 'Morning Stretch Aerobics' group. Sometimes the nursing crew would join me and exercise to the booming Motown music. When all of our ample asses were bent over swaying to the beat, it was difficult to distinguish who was staying in the Psych. Ward. and who was actually getting paid to be there.

"Ethel Marie Clementine, would you like to lead us in a stretch of your choice?"

In a spot on Valley girl voice, Ms. Clementine responded,

"I would like us to stretch our carnival arms and our flesh eating virginias all the way to the floor so like our finger tips and our Volvos drive us hard into super sonic power drills and we jackhammer through the concrete down to like whatever the middle of the Earth where we rescue Toto, Hobbit, and Minnie Pearl."

"Thank you for that stretch, Ethel Marie."

On warm sunny days I would invite everyone outside so they could enjoy the garden and participate in some cool recreational activities. A new patient, Mr. Percival Scrotcher, seemed to have his eyes piercingly focused on my chest or was it on my beach volleyball? I was informed that Percival had special needs and was on constant observation for unpredictable behavior. A group of us began to toss the plastic ball around, lobbing it high, trying to keep it aloft in the air. When it came close to Mr. Scrotcher, he lunged and slapped the whirling sphere forcefully into my groin! Wasn't it fun to watch your own scrotum triple in size? I recovered and started to inflate the beach ball so we could continue.

When Percival noticed me blowing air into our deflated sagging ball, he darted to my side and screamed into my ear, "Mama. Teetee. Mama. Teetee!"

He then popped the ball with his teeth and began grasping what would become known as my ever expanding man nipples.

I spoke loudly and authoritatively, "Stop that, Mr. Scrotcher. I am NOT your mama and these are not your teetees!"

The Psych. Techs. once again rescued me. I quickly heeded Nurse Fontella's words of wisdom and hauled ass with my office keys, sore balls and lilac titties in tow.

After passing my probationary period, I called mother to share some of my unusual work experiences. She inquired, "Honey lamb, what kind of University classes are you teaching and who on Earth are these students?"

I answered, "I'm no longer at the college, mom. Can we say ***PSYCH. Ward?***"

“Things that work my last Gay nerve in New York City!”

Seeing Broadway musicals which have been intentionally scaled down. It is not my fondest wish to see the above-the-title star to simultaneously play the leading role and the tuba on stage! Hi, I saw the original 32 piece orchestra production which won 9 Tonys. *Raise it up*, revival.

Living in Manhattan, the world’s fiercest city that can weather terrorist attacks, Wall Street collapses and 500,000 incessantly pooping canines, but can’t seem to be capable of keeping the sidewalks and thoroughfares free from a wintry mix of sleet, snow and soot colored icy slush. *Got shovel?*

Having more rats in the Subway than people. These rats are ravenous New Yorkers with waist sizes > 40!

Walking across East 85th street only to be struck down by a harried Guatemalan boy who sped away on bicycle to safely deliver his spicy Caribbean combination plate.

Having a roommate in a spacious rent stabilized two bedroom apartment casually mention to you after signing a two year lease and paying 3 months rental deposit that he has developed ‘Part-timers disease’: “Part time I remember to turn off the gas and part time I don’t!”

Tourists who walk around this overcrowded city with umbrellas the size of helicopter landing pads. Unless you are auditioning for the lead in 'Mary Poppins' or attempting to orbit the Hudson, then *SHUT IT DOWN!*

While taking the M-15 downtown, accidentally stepping on the train of a Cambodian woman's loose fitting ankle length skirt, prompting it to unravel and fall to the floor of the crowded city bus, leaving her red faced and bare girdled. Oh, my stars!

Being invited to dinner by a wealthy (and ultra cheap) Manhattan socialite who drinks more vodka than Poland and then suddenly decides at the last moment to 'go Dutch' with the bill. *She's done.*

Those who attend Broadway shows who appear to be more suitably dressed for Barnum & Bailey and who scarf pieces of dripping fried chicken during the performance.

New York City cab drivers who refuse to drive to other boroughs. A. It's the law, mess! B. Haven't they heard that Brooklyn is the *new* Manhattan?

People who travel all the way to Manhattan for the quint-essential New York experience and choose to dine at a charming Times Square fast food chain. P.S.: Get thyself to Orlando.

Living in New York City, running out of opiates and it's only Tuesday.

Flying to New York to see your idol Carol Burnett in a Stephen Sondheim Broadway musical only to be treated to its' sub, Kathie Lee.

Being bombarded on cramped city sidewalks with double decker baby strollers the size of moving vans.

My first Manhattan roommate who chose to keep his collection of triple wrapped condom ready Sudan sized dildoes and fleet of enema douche bags hanging upside down along the chartreuse shower curtain in our shared bathroom.

Musicals that have adopted the tired ass trend of using motion picture screens and images on the stage. If I wanted a movie I would have paid $12.50 instead of a $136 orchestra seat! *Dearest Broadway, may I have a set please?*

Cab drivers who appear unable to navigate the West Village. Note: Competent navigation is the only requirement of your profession. Imagine going to a florist who doesn't do flowers. Hello? How do you spell *GPS*?

Being dragged to the prestigious Metropolitan Opera only to be subjected to its' resident soprano diva warble her quite distinctive way through Puccini, sounding like a vocal apocalypse in which the Cowardly Lion shrieks while tweaked on crystal methamphetamine.

Taking the Subway when it is packed to the brim with bicycles, religious zealots, break dancers, Mariachi bands with enough luggage to clothe Guadalajara, and an assortment of creatures who are unaccustomed to the practice of bathing.

Living next door to the only building crane disaster in Manhattan in the past 50 years. After being advised by one's physician to move due to the neighborhood's current poor air quality and having chronic asthma, you relocate three miles north to the Upper East Side. Five days later, the building across the street from you is also swiftly craned to the ground, sending billows of ash, smoke, and flying debris to your balcony. *Please do not move to my neighborhood.*

While relaxing in Riverside Park, being approached by a stranger riding a 10 speed mountain bike who interrupts your cell phone call and inquires, "Can I have $5 for lunch?", to which you respond, "well, yes, that's *my* lunch." Welcome to the modern world of drive-by panhandling.

Immigrants who have lived in New York City for a quarter century and speak approximately 8 words of English! (please read the chapter, "You're Not in *Bangladesh*, anymore!")

BOROUGHS!

WHITE SQUIRREL WORD SEARCH CAST OF CHARACTERS

CAN YOU FIND THE NUTS HIDDEN BELOW?

A I C N I V O R P E

S A D R E F G N L N

F T Y R E N E O N Y

O A A G L E H R I E

O N E I S T O M K R

P I B K R E S A R T

R P N A G L A H E U

E E W R S L D E M O

T N S L D U N D A S

O E D O A M I N D Y

O L G T F E R H R E

C E A T K A R L Y O

M D H A R R O M O G

TYRENE

COOTERPOOF

PROVINCIA

DELENE PINATA

MINDY MULLET

MERKIN

KARLOTTA

GOMORRAH

DUNDAS

WARTHOLE

HELGA

ENYERT

NORMA

WHITE SQUIRREL WORD SEARCH

DID ALL YOU SQUIRRELS GET THE RIGHT ANSWERS?

A	I	C	N	I	V	O	R	P	E
S	A	D	R	E	F	G	N	L	N
F	T	Y	R	E	N	E	O	N	Y
O	A	A	G	L	E	H	R	I	E
O	N	E	I	S	T	O	M	K	R
P	I	B	K	R	E	S	A	R	T
R	P	N	A	G	L	A	H	E	U
E	E	W	R	S	L	D	E	M	O
T	N	S	L	D	U	N	D	A	S
O	E	D	O	A	M	I	N	D	Y
O	L	G	T	F	E	R	H	R	E
C	E	A	T	K	A	R	L	Y	O
M	D	H	A	R	R	O	M	O	G

"Cheater Cheater, *Compulsive Eater!*"

When your three favorite words in the English language are "Hot Donuts Now", it's a fair conclusion that you are a food addict like me. I am officially obsessed with all things consumable. I don't remember when my insatiable carbohydrate insanity began but it seems like I have been dieting since my ten pound exodus from the womb. While most toddlers' first spoken words are 'mama' and 'dada', mine were 'sour cream'. In Jr. High School I failed gymnastics as I could never master a somersault due to my Olympic regulation basketball sized stomach getting in the way. By college I had tried every imaginable diet and managed to go up and down the scales more times than the Three Tenors. The clothes in my closet looked like an expandable rack at Fat Alberts with sixteen different waist sizes.

I read a bunch of self-help books like "A Return to Carbs" and "You are what you throw up to be." I felt inspired to give up something simple like sugar for the summer. As recommended, I would drink a glass of water each time a craving would unleash a tempting spell upon me. By September I had lost an amazing 40 pounds! I had finally found weight loss Nirvana and could actually fit into my jeans.

Since refined white sugar was no longer a part of my palate, I decided to conduct a personal experiment to prove beyond a shadow of a doubt I had conquered my lifelong addiction. So I journeyed to the nearest donut pub to test my will power. While waiting in line to order, I was offered a free glazed sample. I inhaled it so fast I wasn't certain if

I had really eaten it. Was this an illusion? To ensure that my brain wasn't playing tricks on me, I ordered a dozen more. I scarfed those suckers down in a frenzy. This was confectionary crack and I was its ultimate dope fiend. By Thanksgiving I had gained back all the weight I had lost and then some. I was ecstatic.

I sought professional help from a holistic dietician named Ellen Nellypoot. She took my food intake history for the past month and the various unsuccessful attempts to reach my desired goal weight. Ms. Nellypoot analyzed her critical nutritional findings. "Dear challenged one, if you continue to eat and purge, stuff and starve at your current rate, you will need to be buried inside a concert grand piano case."

This got my attention. Nellypoot elaborated, "Wake up from the Dark Ages deary. You are an extremely emotional eater. If you are happy, you eat. If you are sad, you eat. If you are furious, you eat. Name the emotion, dip it in chocolate fondue and you will suck it down like there's no tomorrow! Am I not spot on?"

I had to admit she was right. Food was my solution for everything. Whatever the occasion, I was first in line to eat it. Ms. Nellypoot referred me to a wellness therapist named Doris Dawandu.

Mrs. Dawandu advised, "First of all, never trust an industry whose first three letters are D-I-E! When you stop eating, you die. You must remember that every meal is not your Last Supper. You are not on death row."

"Ain't that the truth!"

"Second, you are not designed to be a circus freak of nature human yo-yo. Every deprivation leads to an equal or greater binge. You deprived yourself for an entire season of sugar then you literally ate your weight in it!"

I answered, "You are so right. I became quite depressed after topping the scales at 250. My gut grew so large that while showering I was visually unable to determine my own gender. The last time I crashed dieted I lost the weight disproportionately to the point where my belly caved in and my titties started to sprout and kept on growing! My right tit cup size exceeded most of the women I had dated. My hooters became so developed I could feel myself up. Who needed a damn date?"

Doris Dawundu smiled, "Child of Twinkie and Ho Ho, you who never met a sweet treat he didn't eat, the truth will set you free and so will a muzzle, duct tape, refrigerator padlock and stomach stapler. You can either learn to "Eat to Live" and be healthy or "Live to Eat" and be the size of Bora Bora! The choice is yours." While I did desire to live on an island, I did not wish to be bigger than the entirety of its land mass.

I sought assistance from a renowned weight loss hypnotist, Swami Priya Swampwot, who swore my unresolved past life karma was the real reason for my layers of blubber.

Swami Swampwot explained, "Dearest Soul, it matters not if you eat the entire planet every day. Food has nothing to do with your weight whatsoever! It is the inner world within your celestial chakras that desperately desires to be realigned. You are like an enormous engine that needs a major overhaul. Your karmic debt is expressing itself through your fatty tissues. Your poop is shapeless because you have lost your intestinal fortitude. Your torso is gargantuan because you failed to listen to your gut. Do you get what I am telling you, my wondrous Spirit from Ali Baba?"

"I'm clinically obese because I'm a metaphysical mess?"

"Exactly! Just buy my divinely inspired specially priced hypnosis tapes and play them daily. Eat whatever you want and by the end of this year you will be transformed into your higher skinny self. It will be effortless. Surrender your doubt and watch the fat get out!"

That was a catchy mantra! At the exact moment I wrote the humungous check to my new guru, her crystal ball crashed to the floor and shattered everywhere. Swami grinned, "You are cracking through to a brand new you!"

Good to know. One year later and the only things I had cracked were my zippers, bank accounts, and the digital weight scale which miraculously tipped at an all time high. I called to ask what I had been doing wrong since I had failed to get my guaranteed results. Apparently I had been playing Swami Swampwot's hypnosis tapes in reverse. *Who knew?*

CPSIA information can be obtained
at www.ICGtesting.com
Printed in the USA
LVHW090207020119
602415LV00002B/7/P

9 781452 026541